Leslie's Journal

Allan Stratton

annick press

Annick Press Ltd.

Edited by Barbara Pulling
Copy edited and proofread by Heather Sangster
Cover design by Lisa Hemingway

We acknowledge the support of the Canada Council for the Arts, the Ontario Arts Council, and the Government of Canada through the Book Publishing Industry Development Program (BPIDP) for our publishing activities.

 ONTARIO ARTS COUNCIL
CONSEIL DES ARTS DE L'ONTARIO

Cataloguing in Publication

Stratton, Allan
 Leslie's journal : a novel / by Allan Stratton. — Rev. ed.

Originally published 2000.
ISBN 978-1-55451-149-5 (bound).—ISBN 978-1-55451-148-8 (pbk.)

 I. Title.

PS8587.T723L47 2008   jC813'.54   C2008-901860-5

Printed and bound in Canada

Published in the U.S.A. by	**Distributed in Canada by**	**Distributed in the U.S.A. by**
Annick Press (U.S.) Ltd.	Firefly Books Ltd.	Firefly Books (U.S.) Inc.
	66 Leek Crescent	P.O. Box 1338
	Richmond Hill, ON	Ellicott Station
	L4B 1H1	Buffalo, NY 14205

Visit our website at www.annickpress.com

for my students

One

It's only the first week and already school sucks. I've got Ms. Graham again for English.

Today she said every class is going to start with fifteen minutes of journal writing, which is what we're doing now. This is supposed to train us to "reflect freely on our personal experiences." Oh yeah? It's to give her fifteen minutes with nothing to do.

Also, since our journals will be about personal feelings, she says she won't read them. "Your journal is just for you. So write, write, write. As with everything in this world, you'll get out of it what you put into it." According to her, this is a "Life Lesson." What it *really* is is an excuse for her to get out of marking.

A year of journals! Can I scream yet? It's so boring I keep forgetting to breathe. And each day when it's over she's going to collect them and lock them up in her filing cabinet, like we're a bunch of babies who'll lose them or something.

But okay. Journals beat having her teach. Last year, she either read aloud to us or we read aloud to her, then she'd stop and ask us stupid questions about what we'd just heard. This last part was hilarious, because nobody ever gave her an answer. We just stared up at her like we were dead and watched her eyes go funny. No kidding, her eyes were like gerbils. They darted around desperate for a hand to pop in the air till the silence got so bad she couldn't stand it anymore and blurted the answer herself.

Normal teachers would figure if students are passed out, maybe they should do something. LIKE, HELLO, MAYBE STOP ASKING DUMB QUESTIONS! But not Ms. Graham. She went from dumb to dumber. There'd be red patches on her neck and she'd be sweating and wiping the sweat from her hands to her dress. It was disgusting.

That's when she'd tell us to read the next chapter silently and answer the questions on handouts she'd pass around for homework. Which of course we never did. We pretended we hadn't heard her and the handouts didn't exist. At the end of class, we'd crumple them into balls and toss them in the general direction of the wastebasket. It's like, whole rain forests got clear-cut so Ms. Graham could stuff her filing cabinet with handouts that all ended up in the garbage.

Then, pretty soon, we pretended Ms. Graham didn't exist either. We'd come in, put our heads on our desks and go to sleep. Which was fine by her, I guess, because at least if we were sleeping we weren't throwing chalk. Or handouts.

Leslie's Journal

Allan Stratton

annick press

Annick Press Ltd.

Edited by Barbara Pulling
Copy edited and proofread by Heather Sangster
Cover design by Lisa Hemingway

We acknowledge the support of the Canada Council for the Arts, the Ontario Arts Council, and the Government of Canada through the Book Publishing Industry Development Program (BPIDP) for our publishing activities.

ONTARIO ARTS COUNCIL
CONSEIL DES ARTS DE L'ONTARIO

Cataloguing in Publication

Stratton, Allan
    Leslie's journal : a novel / by Allan Stratton. — Rev. ed.

Originally published 2000.
ISBN 978-1-55451-149-5 (bound).—ISBN 978-1-55451-148-8 (pbk.)

    I. Title.

PS8587.T723L47 2008   jC813'.54   C2008-901860-5

Printed and bound in Canada

Published in the U.S.A. by	**Distributed in Canada by**	**Distributed in the U.S.A. by**
Annick Press (U.S.) Ltd.	Firefly Books Ltd.	Firefly Books (U.S.) Inc.
	66 Leek Crescent	P.O. Box 1338
	Richmond Hill, ON	Ellicott Station
	L4B 1H1	Buffalo, NY 14205

Visit our website at www.annickpress.com

for my students

It was sooo painful.

Near the end of the year, she went Missing in Action. They said she was away with chronic bronchitis, but we figured she was having a breakdown. Over the summer the story went around that she'd knocked over a shelf of light fixtures at Wal-Mart and ended up under a pile of lampshades babbling hysterically while trying to strangle herself with an electric cord till the ambulance came and hauled her off in a straitjacket.

Well, that's the rumor. And even if it isn't true, it should be, because obviously she's back for more and she's nutty as ever. Right now she's floating around with this vague look, smelling kind of stale in a pale gray billowy thing. She looks like a human dustball. Wait. She's just come to rest in front of the window. She's looking out. Maybe she's thinking of jumping.

It's kind of sad, really. I mean, if she wasn't a teacher, I'd feel sorry for her. Once upon a time she was somebody's baby, playing patty-cakes and having everybody kissing her and saying she was a cutie. Then she grew up. I picture her all alone in some tiny apartment, surrounded by cats and stacks of unmarked assignments, praying that tomorrow will be better. And it never is.

Poor Ms. Graham. It's not like she wants to be boring. That's why I almost feel guilty when we torture her. Who we *should* torture—really, really torture, with hot coals and a pair of hedge clippers—is Nicky Wicks. He has short greasy hair, cystic acne and a squishy tongue he likes to stick in girls' ears for a joke. He also has a dent in his forehead from where somebody hit him with a shovel when he was little. Too bad they didn't hit harder.

Nicky is the grossest pig in the school, and in this school there's a lot of competition. He only has one redeeming feature. If you want to lose weight, think about making out with him. You won't be able to eat for a week.

Anyway, Nicky "Pus-head" Wicks worked it so he sits one seat ahead of me in three separate classes. What's worse, he apparently thinks it is majorly funny to stick a couple of pencils up his nose and pretend to be a walrus. The real reason he does this is to have an excuse to let his pencils fall on the floor so he can bend down to pick them up and look up my skirt while he's at it.

Today I got my revenge. I waited till lunch, when I knew he'd be in the cafeteria with lots of people all around. Then I marched up to his table and said in a big loud voice, "Hey, Pus-head, you look up my skirt one more time and I'll personally pop your zits with my nail file!"

There was this roar of laughter, hooting and foot-stomping. Nicky was so embarrassed, I thought his cysts would explode. As for me, I just snapped my fingers and diva-ed my way to the parking lot for a smoke.

That's where I met the vice-principal, Mr. Manley, out on a little narc duty. "I want to see you in my office, young lady."

Sorry, journal, according to Ms. Graham it's time for

you to go into the filing cabinet. Tomorrow, I'll tell you what happened with the Nazi.

P.S. Dear Ms. Graham: You promised our journals were going to be private. So in case you're secretly reading this to get some cheap thrills, you are nothing but a crazy perverted liar, and it's not my fault if it sends you over the edge.

Two

Vice-principals are basically school cops. They like to act tough and eat donuts. So, all things considered, I guess Mr. Manley is in the right job. Mr. Manley. Right. As in: "He is so manly." An elephant in a suit is more like it. They say that once upon a time he used to be a phys ed teacher. Now the only exercise he gets is yelling. His vocal cords are on steroids.

It's pathetic. Mr. Manley walks around all tough and important, like he's the FBI or something, when all he really is is some old guy who gets his kicks busting teenagers. I mean, he spends his whole life sneaking behind cars in the school parking lot to catch smokers, or smelling kids' breath for alcohol or pot, or going around with a flashlight at school dances to make sure nobody's having sex on the football field or under the stairwells. What kind of pervert gets off on that?

Last year, in grade nine, Mr. Manley was always hauling me down to his office. I practically lived there. I joked he kept wanting to see me because he had the hots for me, but really it was on account of me being late and skipping all the time. My parents had started this "trial separation" and I wasn't taking it so well.

I'm still not. Especially since it stopped being a "trial," and Mom went from Still-Married-Sort-Of to Officially-Designated-Single-Mother. Now when she sees politicians on TV going on about single moms she starts to cry. Then she yells at me. It's like she's afraid if she doesn't crack down I'm going to turn into this demon seed from a broken home, end up on some talk show maybe. "You're going to improve your behavior," she yells. "Do you hear me, Leslie?"

"No. I'm deaf."

"Cut the attitude!"

I give her the look. She goes ballistic. "Don't give me that look."

"Then stop yelling at me. I mean, no wonder Dad left."

That's when her face goes white and she runs to her room and makes these awful animal sounds. And I want to die. I don't want to hurt her. Really. I just don't want her to yell at me all the time. Why does everything have to be my fault?

Last year after Dad left was pretty bad. I couldn't be around anybody. Sometimes I took off to the mall to see how many movies I could sneak into at the multiplex, or to watch music videos on the wall of big-screen TVs at Laserama Electronics, or to panhandle beside the bank machine to see if I could make a living if I ever had to run away from home. But mostly I just hung out in the far cubicle of the girls' washroom on the second floor east wing and cried.

Needless to say, whenever I did show up for class there was a note telling me to report to the vice-principal. In fact, me getting hauled down to the office turned into what my drama teacher would call a "Ritual."

At first Mr. Manley tried to smarten me up by giving me after-school detentions. No way for that. So guess what he'd do when I'd skip detentions? Give me two-day suspensions. Is that funny or what? I skip school and my punishment is that I get to skip more school. Mr. Manley is a genius in the Stupid Department.

Which brings me back to getting caught in the parking lot. It turns out Brainiac hadn't seen my cigarette after all. Instead, he wanted to talk to me about my "inappropriate dress."

"It's not inappropriate," I say when we're in his office. "It's retro." What it really is is a black vinyl micro-mini with fishnets, platforms and a crop top. Since last May I'm happy to say I haven't needed padding.

"You know what I'm getting at," Mr. Manley snaps back, all eyebrows.

"I'm afraid I don't." I smile sweetly. "Perhaps you'd

like to explain it to me." Teachers hate that smile, because they know exactly what I'm thinking but they can't do anything.

Mr. Manley gives me his famous silent routine. It's deadly. He stares down at a person without any expression, like they're a bug or something, and he just keeps staring. Finally the person goes crazy and starts to twitch. That's when he has them.

Well, he doesn't have me. Last year, maybe, when I was a niner who thought getting sent to the office meant something. But I've been called down so much by now I'm inoculated. Instead of getting scared, I look him straight in the eye. "Mr. Manley, are you saying I look like a slut?"

"That's not what I said," he chokes.

"But it's what you meant, isn't it? Unfortunately, I'm only a junior. I don't know anything about sluts. Perhaps you could tell me about them. For instance, how exactly do sluts dress?" (And here I give him an even sweeter smile.) "In your experience."

We stare at each other hard, him really trying to break me down, me keeping cool by counting his nose hairs. Mr. Manley has hair growing out of his nose and his ears and all over the back of his hands and fingers. I picture him naked. I nearly barf.

Suddenly, for a split second, he looks away. I win. "You will go home, change and report back to this office when you're decent," he mutters. "That will be all."

Go home? I don't think so. I have some baggy clothes in my locker I can put on. They're what I leave the apartment in; otherwise, Mom wouldn't let me out the door. I wear them over top, take them off as soon as I get in the elevator and stuff them in a plastic bag. It sounds dumb, but it saves a fight, and we fight enough as it is.

I tilt my head, smile at Mr. Manley, get up and roll my eyes. "Have a nice day."

I step out into the main office. There's this senior lounging on the counter waiting for a secretary. I walk towards the hall staring straight ahead, but I can tell his eyes are following me. Not just following me—they're burning into the back of my head.

At the doorway, I stop and turn. "What's your damage?"

I expect him to go all red. But he grins, winks and keeps staring. I give him the finger, toss my hair and make an exit.

What a jerk!

Three

Katie was shocked when I told her what I said to Mr. Manley.

Katie is always shocked. That's one of the things I like best about her. Whenever I'm bored, I go up to her and say, "Hey, Katie, guess what I just did?" and before I can say a word her eyes are so wide they look like they're going to fall out of her head.

Katie's been my best friend since I moved to this pit six years ago because of Dad getting transferred. I arrived in October. Everyone was already into their little cliques, and when I was introduced to the class it was like somebody'd farted.

At recess, no one would talk to me. All the boys wanted to do was run around like a bunch of morons screaming their heads off. But the girls—they were just plain mean. They were all in groups acting cute and when I'd come over they'd turn their backs on me and start to whisper and laugh. Mom had made me wear this brand-new outfit with a sweater vest. Nobody else was wearing sweater vests, though, because apparently the Fashion Police had decided they were against the law or something.

Anyway, there I was, feeling like a giant dog turd. I knew I couldn't cry—that would be too embarrassing. So instead I acted like I had something very important to do and marched off the asphalt to the fence at the back of the school yard.

There was a girl there with big cheeks and glasses, sitting under a tree, reading a Harry Potter book. She looked pretty normal, except she was moving her lips. So I sat down about twenty feet from her and pretended to stare at this anthill, like I was a member of the junior science club or something. What I was really doing was praying my dad would get fired so we could move back home where I at least had a few friends. (I can hardly remember their names anymore, except for Laura Wilson, who stopped calling me after three lousy months—even though she'd sworn eternal friendship on her cat Fluffball's grave.)

I was just about to lose it when I heard a voice. "Oh, hi. You're Leslie, right?" I looked over and it was Moving-Lips Girl. "I'm sorry for being so rude," she went on. "It's just that Harry's in the middle of a spell and I didn't even see you come over."

I shrugged as if I didn't care one way or the other.

"My name's Katie. I sit three rows over from you. Where are you from?"

"Seattle."

"Seattle? But that's in the United States!" Her eyes went all big, like this was the most amazing thing she'd ever heard, and we've been best friends ever since.

I love Katie. I couldn't have made it through last year without her. During the stuff with my parents—the yelling, the fights, the separation—she was always ready to listen or make me laugh. Even when her mother told her to get off the phone—"It's Family Hour, Katie!"—I knew she'd find a way to sneak to the basement wash-room and call me back on her cell. And for Katie, calling back after getting the Word is a big deal.

Katie is what adults call "well behaved"—which they apparently think is a compliment. Personally, I call "well behaved" being a suck, and it's the one thing about Katie that sometimes bugs me. Luckily, Katie *knows* she's a suck. "I just can't help myself," she laughs, eyes bulging. So how can I stay mad? I mean, "I can't help myself" is exactly what I say, only about getting in trouble.

I guess that's why we're friends: we forgive each other. Katie says when she looks at me she sees a terrific person who really wants to do good. I say that when I look at her I see a spawn of Satan who really wants to cut loose. I'm not totally teasing. The reason Katie loves to be shocked by my stories is because I do and say the stuff she can't.

Katie's biggest problem is her mother. Mrs. Kincaid is this giant spider sucking the life out of her. She's this giant slug oozing slime. She's this—don't get me started!

Let's just say that Mrs. Kincaid thinks everyone and everything should be nice. As in "Don't you look nice!" Or lovely. As in "Don't you look lovely!" Or just about perfect. As in "Don't you look just about perfect!" Not perfect, mind you. Just about perfect. That's because she thinks the only perfect one is her. Naturally, Mrs. Kincaid doesn't think I'm nice or lovely or anywhere close to being just about perfect. What Mrs. Kincaid thinks I am is trouble. As in "Leslie Phillips is nothing but trouble." That's what I heard her say to Mr. Kincaid one night last year when she thought me and Katie were down in the rec room watching TV.

At first I was hurt. I'd always thought she liked me. But obviously things had changed since my parents' separation and the move into our dump of an apartment and me starting to go wild. "Acting out" is how our family counselor put it when I got caught sneaking home drunk. To hear my mom tell it, you'd have thought I was an alcoholic or something.

"But you're only in grade nine!"

"Yeah, well, I'm fourteen, so get used to it."

That's when the counselor said I was "acting out." "How would you know?" I yelled. "You're just some turd. Get flushed, why don't you?" I never went back.

Anyway, I decided I didn't have to care what Mrs. Kincaid thought. After all, I was Katie's friend, not hers. At least that's what I figured till Katie phoned last year at the end of spring break and said we had to talk.

"But we always talk," I said. "We're talking right now."

"This is different. We have to talk in private."

"Well, this is private. Unless your mother's listening in again. Hello, Mrs. Kincaid, isn't it a lovely day out? Why, I'd say it's just about perfect."

"Cut it out, Leslie. I'm serious. We really have to talk. In person."

My heart started thumping because Katie was sounding so weird. I imagined maybe she had some kind of terrible disease or her parents had been killed in a car crash. We decided to meet at two o'clock at my place, because my mom would be out doing groceries. After we hung up, I just sat there shaking, thinking of how I'd have to act brave and comfort her.

But when Katie arrived she didn't look sick or anything. Just sort of fidgety. And she smiled a lot, really fake, and said, no, she was fine and her parents were fine and wasn't spring break great and they should give a prize to whoever invented it.

"Cut the crap, Katie," I said. "I've been worried sick all day. What's the deal with this Having to Talk? In Person. In Private."

"Well ..." She took a deep breath and started scrunching her knees and staring at the coffee table. "My mom ..."

"Yeah? Your mom what?"

"My mom thinks we shouldn't spend so much time together."

My stomach went hollow. "Why? Is she afraid we're turning into lesbians or something?"

"No."

"Well, so what if we were? Your mom is a bigot."

"No, she isn't."

"Yes, she is." I gulped for air. "She hates me."

"She says we should expand our circle of friends."

"Yeah, right. That's just a nice way of saying, 'I think you should stop seeing Leslie.'"

"It is not."

"Besides, I don't want to 'expand my circle of friends.' I want things the way they are."

Katie started flapping her hands and looking at me

all helpless like she always does when her mom means business.

"It's not fair. First Dad runs out on me. And now you."

"I'm not running out on you."

"You are so."

Suddenly I couldn't take it anymore and started to sob. Without even thinking, Katie gave me a big hug and I hugged her back and we didn't let go. When I settled down, she took my head in both hands and stared deep into my eyes. "Leslie," she said, "you're my best friend in the whole world. And you'll always be my best friend. Cross my heart."

Katie looked so serious and sweet I wanted to cry all over again. But instead I started to giggle. And then she started to giggle too. Before we knew it, we were both rolling around laughing and everything seemed okay again.

But Mrs. Kincaid meant business: Never trust a mother who smells like hair spray. Our first day back after the spring break, she had Katie hand out invitations to a sleepover. Naturally I got one too—Mrs. Kincaid was too smart to make Katie take me off the list. But it was all part of her master plan. Because instead of Katie and me doing something fun on our own, we'd be with a bunch of other girls. Other girls who hate me and make me feel left out.

Head of the Leaving-Me-Out Department is Ashley Walker. She goes to Katie's church, and ever since that first sleepover she's butted into our friendship. She makes Katie feel guilty if she doesn't participate in their stupid youth group activities. So instead of doing stuff with me on the weekend, half the time Katie ends up being Ashley's buddy at some charity car wash or geeky youth wiener roast.

Katie even made me come and hear her and Ashley the first time they performed in the church's junior choir. I almost puked watching Ashley flounce around in her polyester choir robe, like she was a big deal or something.

Last summer was worst of all. Ashley got Katie to go with her to the church youth leadership training camp, so for two whole weeks I was stuck on my own. "You could've come," Katie said. "The youth group's always looking for new members."

Yeah, right. New members who are nice and lovely and just about perfect.

God, I hate Ashley. I told Katie, but she said I shouldn't be mean because Ashley has problems too.

"Like what?"

"Dermatitis."

"Dermatitis?" I laughed. "You mean she's all scaly."

"Leslie, don't make me choose sides."

"Is that a warning?"

"Just don't." Katie turned on her heel and walked off. I felt lost. She never used to get mad at me. What happened?

Life doesn't make sense. It's against the law for somebody to steal your bike, but apparently it doesn't matter if somebody tries to steal your best friend. Well, you can always get a new bike. But how do you replace a best friend?

Four

Today is Friday. At lunch I go into the cafeteria, and see Katie and Ashley A-hole with a bunch of other girls clumped by the window. Katie and I used to have lunch alone, only now her table's turned into Girl Central. They're always in a group, pointing and whispering and generally being embarrassing. Right now, they're staring at the track.

"What's the big deal?" I say.

"Leslie, look. By the goalposts," squeals Katie. "He's just transferred and his name is Jason McCready and he's a senior and he has a motorcycle and ohmigod!" She sighs and does this fake fainting routine like I'm supposed to be impressed she's got hormones.

When I look out, I see it's him, the guy from the office. And come to think of it, he *is* pretty cute, slouched all alone against the goalpost, one knee slightly bent, hands in his back pockets, head back to catch some rays. He looks like an underwear model with clothes on.

"Oh, him," I say casually, as I stuff my face with

the last bit of my tuna sandwich. "We've already met."

"No way."

"Not my type," I yawn, and I turn away like he's the last thing on my mind.

"Liar," Ashley sneers. "I'll bet you've never even seen him before."

"Oh, no? Well, I've not only seen him before, I've given him the finger."

Katie gasps. "What did he do?" Her eyes are like pies.

"Nothing. He just smiled."

Katie is in awe. "Smiled? You mean he likes you?"

The idea hadn't crossed my mind, but I'm not going to say no and look stupid in front of Ashley. So instead, I check my nails. "Some of us have what it takes."

"Liar," Ashley sneers. "If you and Jason are such good friends, let's see you go out and talk to him. He'll tell you to get lost."

I'm trapped. But I'm not going to let Ashley show me up.

"Candy from a baby," I laugh, and I head out to the track, praying by the time I get there he'll be gone.

He isn't. When I get within range, I slow down. Stop. I can tell he knows someone's there, but he keeps his eyes closed and lets the breeze play through his curly brown hair. His shirt's hanging out and open, and under it he's got on this incredibly tight T-shirt. Can I breathe?

I can feel the girls stare at me. There's no turning back. "Hi. You must be Jason."

A pause. "If you say so." His eyes are still closed.

"We, uh, we met in the office."

He opens his eyes. They are sooo blue. "Then you must be the principal."

For a second, I don't get it. "Uh ..." I want to run. But I'm frozen.

"Are those your friends?" He nods towards the caf.

The girls have their faces squashed against the window like they're in kindergarten. They look demento, especially Katie, who's waving her hand so fast I'm surprised it doesn't fall off.

"Friends? I've never seen them before."

He smiles. His teeth are whiter than white. "Come here."

I take two baby steps, then toss my head and walk right up. Without warning, he puts his arm around me and gives me a kiss. And not just any kiss. He actually slips me the tongue!

He smiles again. "Gotta go," he says.

"Okay." I feel sort of absentminded, like an amnesia patient in some Movie of the Week. My knees are wobbly. I try not to fall down.

"By the way, my name is Leslie," I call after him.

"Right," he says. He waves, real casual and slow, and keeps on walking. I turn to the cafeteria window and curtsy. Katie's eyes are right out of their sockets. Ashley looks like she's just had a heart attack.

And me? I'm in love!

Five

*A*fter school on Friday, I found his locker. On the first floor in the south wing. Number 1124. Just my luck. It's miles away.

Spying on a guy's locker is tricky, because if he finds out, for sure he'll never want to see you again. But this morning I couldn't help myself. All weekend I kept thinking if I wasn't there when Jason arrived, he'd meet some other girl and it'd be all over.

I tried to blend into the walls, walking slowly up and down the corridor, pretending to read *To Kill a Mockingbird*, then stopping for some water at the drinking fountain. Dumb or what? I looked like a browner and I had to pee all morning.

To make matters worse, Jason didn't show. He's not even here today. Maybe he's had an accident. Maybe he's switched schools. Or maybe I'm being stupid, which is probably more like it. I bet he's just skipping, which is what I'd be doing if I wasn't trying so hard to see him.

Jason, Jason, Jason. Love is a killer, especially if you can't talk to anyone about it. Like, if I tell Katie how I feel, she'll tell Ashley and Ashley'll tell the world. As for Mom? Get real. When I'm suicidal she laughs it off as a "phase," and when I'm happy she gets suspicious.

I'm extra obsessed on account of I wanted to see Jason after my shitty weekend. It was Dad's turn to have me, only he was busy Saturday. Fine. He's *always* busy Saturday, working overtime, he says, since Mom is out to nail him in the divorce. (Which she says is a lie, but that's another story.)

To cut it short, Dad picks me up Sunday about two o'clock and tells me today is going to be special—there's a surprise at his apartment. As we drive out to Oakville, I'm thinking, Great, he's finally fixed his old DVD player so we can watch movies instead of being stuck staring at each other over buckets of cold Chinese takeout.

Well, the DVD player isn't the surprise. When he opens the door, I see a couple of empty packing boxes in the hallway, and there's this strange smell of air freshener. Then Dad calls out, "We're home," and all of a sudden she bounces in from the bedroom looking like a Colgate commercial.

Her name is Brenda. I know that without anyone saying, because Mom and Dad used to fight about her all the time before they split up. And now I get to see her, all cute and perky, this overgrown cheerleader out to make a good impression. "Hi," she says, and out comes her hand like she actually expects me to shake it.

"This is the surprise?" I glare at Dad.

Brenda ignores what I think is a pretty obvious signal. "You must be Leslie," she beams.

"And you must be the Bitch," I reply.

Brenda looks like someone just slapped her—if only!—and Dad's ears go red. As per usual, he knows he should say something but can't figure out what, so he just sputters, "Leslie ..."

"No, Dave, it's all right." Brenda pats his arm. "I understand."

Dad settles down and tries his fatherly bit. "Leslie, Brenda's accepted my invitation to move in."

I look at the boxes. I sniff the air. "No kidding."

Now Dad puts his arm around her. My stomach's dissolving.

As for Brenda, she's from another planet. "I'd like to be your friend," she bubbles.

I want to explode, but I don't. Instead, I pin her with my eyes, smile and say in a sweet little voice: "Is that so? Well, if you'd like to be my friend, perhaps you could tell me why you broke up my family and ruined my life?"

"Leslie! You will apologize!" Dad shouts.

"Eat shit!"

Dad looks at Brenda like a deer caught in the headlights. "I'm sorry. I should have told her in the car." The car? He should have told me in the car? Is this my father?

"Take me home! Now!"

I look out the window the whole way back. I don't say a word. All those Saturdays he was so busy with "overtime." What a joke.

Dad stops outside my apartment building. As I open the car door, he clears his throat. Here it comes.

"I'm very disappointed in you, Leslie."

"Is that a fact."

"You embarrassed me. And you embarrassed your-self."

"Whatever." I get out and head up the walk.

"Come back here, young lady! I'm not finished!"

"Oh yes, you are," I think, and I run as fast as I can. I get to the elevator, shoot upstairs. No way he'll follow me. He doesn't have the guts.

"Back so early?" Mom asks. She tries to act casual, but I know she's happy. She's always happy when I come back early. It means I'm mad at Dad. Well, I'm mad at her too. I slam my door, hurl myself on the bed and sob.

There's a little knock. "Honey?"

"Go away."

"What's wrong?"

"Nothing."

"That crying doesn't sound like nothing."

"Just leave me alone."

Leave me alone. That's not asking too much, is it? But does she? No! She opens the door! She starts to come in!

"Honey—"

"I ... SAID ... LEAVE ... ME ... ALONE!!!" And I throw my hairbrush at her. Why does she have to make everything so hard?

I hate this life.

And then I think of Jason. Beautiful, beautiful Jason

with his deep blue eyes and curly brown hair. I picture us gunning down some deserted highway on his motorcycle, me holding on tight around his waist.

Who am I kidding? I'm in love with some guy who probably doesn't even remember I exist.

Six

It's only been a week since we started doing journals, but already a lot of the class have stopped writing. They say they wrote down everything about their life on day one. "But every day is a new adventure!" Ms. Graham exclaimed. Hello? Has she checked the mirror lately?

Anyway, for people with no ideas, she's agreed to post a daily "Topic for Reflection." Today's topic is "What Makes Dreams Come True?" General groan, cuz guess what? They don't. And when they do, you wish they hadn't. Take Ms. Graham. If she ever dreamed of being a teacher, I'll bet she's been kicking herself all the way to her shrink's ever since. And if she dreamed of being anything else, well, I rest my case.

All the same, lame or not, I'm going to write about it, just to stop thinking about You-Know-Who for two seconds. I mean my whole life is thinking about him, which is totally stupid and driving me crazy, but I can't help it. I pretend he's moved to Australia, only right away

I imagine him in tight shorts and a cowboy hat hopping around on a kangaroo. Or I pretend he's dead, only I imagine him in his coffin, all beautiful like he's sleeping, and smelling of lilies. I picture myself kissing a rose and putting it over his heart, so that a little part of me will be with him forever. Sick or what?

Back to the topic. I only know three people who believe in dreams coming true: Mom, Katie and Walt Disney.

Mom says dreams have a catch, though. She says they only come true if you plan ahead and work hard to make them happen. This is why I'm supposed to buckle down and study, so that later on, when "opportunity knocks," I'll be able to answer the door. Not that planning ahead and working hard has done anything for her, other than getting her a divorce, a lousy apartment and temp work. When I remind her of this, she tells me to stop being negative. She says I'm too young to be cynical. I say she's too old not to be.

"But, honey, these are the best years of your life."

"Then shoot me."

This gets her all teary. "Leslie, when you say things like that, I don't know whether to laugh or cry."

So now I'm supposed to feel guilty? No way. "If you're thinking of crying, don't."

Mom apparently believes in the Magical Land of Happy Teenagers where nobody worries about pregnancy, AIDS, gangs or the future, and the most serious thing is a zit before the prom. In the Magical Land of Happy Teenagers there's no STDs or overdoses, and everyone's polite and helpful and smiles like an idiot.

Mom should be committed.

Katie also believes in dreams coming true. According to her, you don't have to work for your dreams, you just have to pray for them. According to her, God answers her prayers all the time.

"Oh yeah?" I say. "Well, He didn't give you that A you wanted in geography."

"Only because I didn't pray hard enough. But He gave me a C, and if I hadn't prayed at all I would have failed."

Katie also believes in God answering prayers because of her teeth. Since forever, she'd been praying for Him to fix her overbite. Finally, at the end of grade eight, her parents took her to an orthodontist, who gave her braces. She showed me this miracle the next morning before school.

"Katie," I said, "are you trying to tell me God is a dentist?"

That made her really mad. She said if God was going to answer her prayers, it was mean for me to get picky about how He did it. In fact, it was a sin. I went to say something smart, but she put her hands over her ears and started to hum some hymn.

"Look, Katie, I believe in God," I yelled, since it was the only thing I figured would shut her up. "I just think

He's got more on His mind than your stupid braces. Making sure the planets don't collide, for one thing."

And suddenly, there in my grade school playground, I had a flash of God as this Cosmic Juggler, and us as billions and trillions of balls He's got in the air. Some of us stay up and some of us fall down. And who stays up and who falls down—well, it all depends on whether He loses His concentration.

Katie liked my theory, except she said God never loses His concentration because He's perfect. She says everything has a reason, and God has a Divine Plan for each and every ball. If a ball falls, either it didn't go where it was supposed to go or God planned for it to fall all along.

Katie's idea of a Divine Plan is what English teachers like Ms. Graham call Destiny. Or Fate. It's why young lovers get together at the end of a story, unless they're in *Romeo and Juliet*, in which case they die.

Mom and Katie are lucky. They really believe there's a reason for everything, and that sooner or later you'll be happy if you just work or pray hard enough. I want to be like them, but lately I've been overcome by this fear. I just start sweating and I think—what if there isn't a plan? What if Destiny is just a fancy word for luck? I mean, what if things just happen because they happen? For no reason at all?

For example, maybe you want to get some chips from the store across the street. But the second you step off the curb you're hit by a truck. For no reason! It just happens!

If things just happen because they happen, then you have no control. You're helpless. We all are. Even parents. There's no one—nothing—to protect us. Not ever.

I don't want that. I want a world that makes sense. Where things have meaning. That's why even though I think Mom and Katie are crazy, I really hope they're right. Because then I can stop worrying. Like, if my dream of Jason and me being together is part of some Divine Plan—if it's destined or something—then it'll just happen. Or if dreams need a little work, I can keep checking his locker. Or if prayer helps ... Well, okay, not that I believe in it or anything, but just in case, *Dear God: If Jason comes up and asks me for a date, I promise to believe in You.*

Am I ever glad no one's reading this.

Seven

God exists! I've been rescued from hell! Okay. First the hell part. Yesterday Katie invited me to another of her Saturday night all-girl sleepovers. I was kind of glad to be asked, because if I hadn't been, I'd be suicidal. But I'm also thinking, hey, we're in grade ten now—aren't we a bit old for this shit? I mean, couldn't we have a house party? But no, at Katie's place there's rules about no cigarettes or booze or boys. Once, as a joke, I asked Katie if I could bring some homemade hash brownies to liven things up. You should have seen her face. It was like I'd invited her to join a Satanic cult.

At Katie's parties, we all sit around in the rec room in our nighties. (Except for me. I usually sleep in my underwear, so Mrs. Kincaid makes me wear an old pair of Katie's pajamas, plastered with kittens or ballerinas. I basically look like a dork, but that's okay so long as nobody takes pictures.) We eat popcorn and chips and play stupid games and gossip. Then Mrs. Kincaid comes down with more so-called treats, like Rice Krispies squares and Jell-O fruit cups, and also stuff she makes from recipes on the backs of packages, like multicolored mini-marshmallows and canned mandarin orange slices in sour cream. I swear: Eat that crap, you'll be puking rainbows.

Anyway, Mrs. Kincaid's got her ear to the air vent the whole night, because the second we bring up the subject of boys she's down again to interrupt with the nutty idea we might like to dye our hair. She hands out these Krazy Kolors that wash out—Krazy Kolors, crazy if you're a clown, maybe—and, bingo, we're all dyeing our hair and giving each other facials and rolling around in hysterics. Ha ha, remind me to laugh. Oh, and did I mention the fashion show? The thrills never stop.

It's not that I don't like facials and fashion shows. Katie and me used to have them all the time. But it was just the two of us. It's different when you do stuff with people who're just putting up with you.

Hearing the hilarity, Mrs. Kincaid comes back and whispers loud in Katie's ear, "Your father's trying to get some work done. How be you girls settle down and watch a movie?" Katie always acts as if this is a great idea and puts on some sucky piece of junk they taped off the Family Channel.

After gagging for five minutes, I suggest we turn down the sound and make up fake dialogue. At which point, Ashley either goes, "Leslie, we're enjoying this. If you aren't, why don't you go home?" or "Come on, Leslie, you're looking for an excuse to say something gross and spoil everything." When I turn to Katie for support she just flaps her hands and looks helpless. I know she doesn't want to choose sides, but her silence sure feels like a choice to me.

I go off in a corner and pretend to read whatever's on the coffee table. I sigh a lot and moan and generally bug everybody till they start throwing cushions at me. Then finally it's midnight, and Mrs. Kincaid comes back down and turns the lights out.

"Sleep tight."

It is always the same and it is always torture!

So when Katie invites me this time I say, "Sure, great," but I'm seriously thinking up excuses to cancel. Until I get home, that is, and find Mom rummaging around my room in Amazon Warrior mode. It seems Mr. Manley has called about my "continued inappropriate dress," and Mom's discovered I'm not wearing what I leave the house in. In fact, I'm wearing clothes she didn't even know I had.

"You're quite a piece of work, Leslie," she fumes, pointing at my secret wardrobe. She's started to dig clothes out of supposedly empty drawers under my bed, and she's throwing them onto a big pile in the middle of the room. "What's the meaning of this?"

How do I answer that? I don't even try. Instead, I point at the "Leslie's Room: Keep Out" sign on the door. "Can't you read?" I yell. "Like, whatever happened to trust?"

Mom shoves the pile into a green garbage bag. "These are going out with the trash."

"Who the hell do you think you are?"

She ignores me, holding up a black bustier. "Where did you get this filth?"

"For your information, that filth just so happens to be a present from Dad." This is partly true, because I bought most of this stuff with money he gave me for Christmas and my birthday. Also with money I borrowed from his wallet. (I don't call it stealing, I call it getting even. He says he gives me money instead of gifts so I can get something I'll really like. Bullshit. He'd rather spend time with precious Brenda than shop for his daughter.)

Anyway, Mom is apparently deaf. She stuffs the last of the clothes into the bag and heads towards the door. "Get out of my way."

"You toss my stuff, next time you're out I'll toss your stuff!"

Mom stops in her tracks. She's so mad I think she's going to have a stroke. "You are sooo grounded!"

"Go ahead. Ground me." I glare back. "If I have to stay home, I'll make your life hell. You up for it?"

For a second, Mom gets this scared look in her eyes. She knows she can't back down. But she knows I won't back down either. Stalemate. That's when I play my ace. I tell her about Katie's sleepover and how Katie was planning to introduce me to some girls from her church youth group. That cools Mom down, seeing as she thinks Katie is such a good influence. "Will her mother be there?"

"What do you think?"

She checks anyway, calling Mrs. Kincaid that very second. To cut a long story short, I'm no longer grounded and the bag of clothes stayed in my room. I should be a diplomat or something.

Which brings me to how God exists after all.

I'm at my locker this morning when I realize I'm being stared at. I turn around, and it's Jason. He doesn't say much. Just smiles and points his finger at me. "I'll be at Mister Pizza's at 12:10." Then he winks, swivels slowly and saunters down the hall.

Katie, Ashley, Kimberly and Sara all stand there dumbstruck, jaws bouncing off the floor. I take off fast so they won't see I feel the same way.

The rest of the morning I spend in the washroom getting ready for our date. I make sure I'm at Mister Pizza's early. But no sooner am I getting comfortable than in waltzes the coven. They sit down at the next booth.

"What are you trying to do, scare him off?" I say.

"You don't own this place," Ashley smirks.

I want to smack her, but then I see Jason crossing the road, so I let out a major sigh and move to the booth at the far end. In he walks all breezy and confident, gives me a nod, goes up to the counter and orders two slices of double cheese, pepperoni and mushrooms and a couple of Cokes. (He knows what I want without even asking—is he amazing or what?) Then he brings them to the table, passing by my so-called friends like they don't exist.

After a little small talk, Jason asks if I'm doing anything Saturday night. I tell him I'll have to check my calendar. He laughs, like he knows there's nothing to check, and says great, he'll pick me up at my place around six. We can grab a quick bite and an early flick, then go to a couple of clubs he likes. I tell him I'll need fake ID, but he says not to worry, he knows the guys at the door. Or if it bothers me, we can go to an all-ages club a few blocks over.

Terrific. Only I suddenly remember he can't pick me up at my place because I'm supposed to be at Katie's, so I tell him I'll be hanging out at the Southside Mall all Saturday afternoon. We arrange to meet at Starbucks. Then he knocks back the rest of his Coke, says, "Catch ya later" and heads out the door.

I get up slow, stretch and glide over to the loser booth. "Guess who's going clubbing with Jason McCready Saturday night?" I gloat.

"But what about my party?" Katie asks.

"Sorry," I say. "Divine intervention."

Katie looks like somebody let the air out of her bicycle tires.

"That's okay," sniffs Ashley. "I guess we know who your real friends are, don't we, Katie?"

I glare at her, but before I can say anything Katie whines, "But my mom's expecting you. What'll I tell her?"

"Say I got sick."

"You want me to lie?"

"Not lie exactly, just help me out."

"I can't lie to my mother."

This calls for heavy artillery. "Look, Katie, if you don't tell your mother I'm sick, I'll tell her about you-know-what."

Katie goes white. You'd think she'd killed somebody or something instead of what she really did, which was have a quickie puff on this joint I scored. (She couldn't even hold it down, just coughed her guts out.) "You promised you'd never tell!"

"Be good and I won't," I smile, and I blow them all a kiss, pirouette and sail away.

Outside, I can't believe what I've done. I've blackmailed my best friend. And I almost don't feel guilty!

Eight

Two days till Saturday. This is worse than waiting for Christmas. Why does time go by so slowly?

Ms. Graham isn't looking too good today. Nicky Wicks has been organizing book drops, and it's getting to her. It all started when Ms. Graham made him sit front-row center where she could "keep an eye on him" because he was always talking. But now everyone can see him, and when her back is turned he gives a signal and the class drop their books on the floor—boom—and watch her jump. She could be in the Olympics. I mean, she jumps so high I'm surprised her head doesn't go through the ceiling. I can just picture it: Ms. Graham trapped up there with her head stuck in the acoustic tiles, kicking her legs while Nicky looks up her dress.

I don't do the book drop thing. Maybe I'm turning into a suck. It's just that even if Ms. Graham is boring, she's basically okay. At least she's not mean, and if we aren't careful she'll get sick again and who knows who we'll get for a supply.

It's *still* two days till Saturday. I'm going crazy sitting here.

I wish I had a cell phone so Jason and I could text each other. It's not like Ms. Graham would notice. But I don't. I'm, like, the only person in the whole world without a cell. I had one before my parents split up, but

Mom says we can't afford it anymore. Dad offered to pay, but she said no. She gave some stupid reason, but the real reason is: If Dad pays, she won't see the bill, or know how often I'm calling and texting him. And she thinks *I'm* selfish and immature.

At least she lets Dad pay for Internet. That's because she wants it too. I'm only allowed on for half an hour a day, unless I'm doing something for school. "That's not enough time to check Facebook and e-mails," I say, which gets me her sermon about the difference between a *real* life and a *virtual* life. Like *she'd* know. I sneak extra time when she's late getting home, but it's hard getting around her. The computer's in the living room so we can share it. I had to go with that or have her in my room all the time.

Hmm. Ms. Graham's at her desk pretending to mark, but her pen isn't moving. Neither are her eyes. She's just staring. I don't think she's going to teach today.

Great. Back to Jason and me. The other girls are sooo impressed. Except, of course, for Ashley A-hole, who goes around pretending she'd never date a senior, that only sluts do that. Eat your heart out is all I can say.

I mean, how could anyone *not* go out with Jason? He's terminally cool. When I see him in the hall he winks, points his finger at me like it's a gun, grins and mouths "Saturday." I wink, point my finger and mouth "Saturday" right back. Then we both walk away like we're spies who've just passed a message in some secret code. Did I say *walk?* It's more like I'm floating.

Weird, eh? I mean, I've never been romantic like this before—not even when I was little and playing with dolls. Back in grade four, Katie's favorite thing was marrying Barbie and Ken and having them go on honeymoons to smoochie places like Niagara Falls or the Bahamas. Except she'd never let them have sex because she said they hadn't been married long enough. Well, no smoochie getaways for me. When it was my turn to pick a honeymoon, I'd have Barbie and Ken go on adventures. They'd scuba in the bathtub. Or skydive off the balcony with napkins taped to their hands for parachutes.

The last time we played honeymoon, Mrs. Kincaid was out getting her hair done, and I had Barbie and Ken go on an African safari in the oven. Katie screamed when they started to melt. "You murdered them!" she cried, holding the dolls in her mother's oven mitts.

It was kind of true. Barbie's eyes were running down her face, and her hair was this goo mixed in with what used to be Ken's feet. But I wasn't about to let that spoil a good honeymoon. "If they're dead, we better give them a funeral," I said. "You can be the minister and say a prayer." The idea of being a minister cheered Katie right up. She gave a long speech about Barbie's good deeds and her tragic love for Ken and then we buried them in the garden. The next week, we dug them up and played Zombie Barbie, but that's another story.

Anyway, with Jason, I finally get what all the fuss is

about. When he kissed me on the football field—well, just thinking about it makes things tingle in a way that's really amazing. Believe it or not, that was my very first French kiss. The truth is, even though I'm fifteen, the only thing I'm experienced at is making stuff up.

Guys don't go for me. I scare them. They like to feel they're in control, but with me, let's face it, they never know what's going to come out of my mouth. (News flash: neither do I.)

This scoop would give Mom a heart attack. Every time I come home late or get caught sneaking out after she's gone to bed, she's certain it's to see some guy. I get back and there she is at the kitchen table in her housecoat. Sometimes she's Volcano Mom ("What have you been up to, young lady?"), but mostly she's Long-Suffering Mom, wiping away tears with a box of Kleenex, trying to make me feel guilty.

Mom is afraid I'm going to end up pregnant. She's especially worried when I come home smelling of beer. "What's his name?" she yells, as if you need a guy to get drunk. All you need is to crash a house party. "Do you know about AIDS? Do you know about condoms?" She throws such big production numbers I swear she oughta be in show business. And she's always leaving magazines around open to stories about the tragedy of teen moms. I think she watches too much *Oprah*.

I want to say, "Look, Mom, stop being so embarrassing." But if she gets off on worrying, let her. Besides, actually talking to her would be awful. She doesn't really want to know about my sex life any more than I want to know about hers.

With other girls, it's trickier. I can't let them think I don't have a boyfriend. So when everybody's talking about their big heartthrob, I invent one. They have names like Jaden and Caleb and Josh and are always mysterious, guys from far away who can be ditched whenever there starts to be too many questions, like when's he going to drop by the school for a visit. When asked how far I've gone, I say, "Wouldn't you like to know?" or "Guess" and let people think I'm this big make-out expert.

Katie's crowd used to come to me for advice, because they've never gone further than sweaty hand-holding and lip kissing. "Frenching!" Katie made a face. "That's so gross. I want to brush my teeth just thinking about it."

But Katie blabbed the truth about me and boys to Ashley last summer, at their stupid youth leadership training camp, and as soon as they got back Ashley ran around and told everybody else. Needless to say, the next time the topic of boys came up and I mentioned I'd met this guy called Ricky at my dad's apartment building, the girls all gave me these funny looks.

Katie turned red and her eyes popped, and right away I knew what had happened. But I didn't crack. Instead, I laughed and said in a really loud voice, "Let me guess—Ashley's pretending to be an expert on my sex life, right?" And then I turned to Ashley and practically shouted. "You are such a pathetic baby, Ashley Walker. Who are you to talk about anybody? You can't even say the word 'penis.' Say it, Ashley! *Penis, penis, penis!*"

Seeing as we were hanging around the mall at the time, I got a lot of attention. I also made Ashley cry. Serves her right after how she treats me. Like, she's lucky I don't blog about her on Facebook. I mean, I wouldn't, but she deserves it.

Getting even with Ashley was one thing, but I still worried about what the other girls thought. That's why Frenching with Jason in broad daylight was extra fantastic.

Jason, you are my dream come true. But now I have something new to worry about: will I be *his* dream come true? He probably thinks I'm experienced, and I'm still wondering how far is too far on a first date.

Worrying about what to do is bad enough. But even worse is worrying about how to do it. Even simple stuff like kissing. That time on the football field doesn't count, because it happened so fast and out of the blue I didn't have a chance to tense up. But knowing it's coming is a different story.

Your reputation can get ruined in one night. Back in grade eight, Rachel Moses didn't do anything the first time she got kissed, just opened her mouth. Ever since, guys have called her "Slug Tongue." And then there's Debby Grace. She bit into Tommy Singh's lip so bad it bled and swelled up. So now she's "Cannibal

Girl." How a person kisses can affect their whole life.

Maybe I should stay home from school tomorrow. That way I can practice kissing in front of the bathroom mirror. Also, I can make sure I don't catch a cold. I mean Saturday has to be perfect, and kissing with a runny nose—well, can you imagine?

Nine

Oh god. It's Wednesday. Four days after my date. I'm in English. And I'm going out of my mind. Every time people laugh, I think it's about me. When I cross the cafeteria, I'm sure the world's staring.

Jason, I have to see you. Did you tell anyone what we did?

I need to know, but he hasn't been at school this week. I've left a zillion messages on his cell—I've e-mailed, too—but he hasn't answered.

Monday morning the girls crowded around me at my locker, all curious. "How was your date with Mister Stud Muffin?"

"Okay," I said.

"Just okay?" All those grinning faces. Had they heard something?

"It was great. We saw a movie, went dancing at some warehouse, no big deal. Why, are you my mother?"

"What's with you?"

"Nothing."

"Well, Katie's party was the best yet," Ashley piped up from nowhere. "No losers to wreck things."

Everyone sucked in their breath, expecting me to punch her or something. I might have, too, only the five-minute bell rang and everyone took off.

Except for me.

I went to my cubicle in the second-floor washroom and thought about my date with Jason, which is all I've been doing since it happened. My mind is like this horror movie on automatic replay. I can't make it stop or go away.

Sleep? Forget it. Last night I snuck one of Mom's pills. Even that didn't help. I'd close my eyes and the movie'd start on the inside of my eyelids. Like, I'm not just having a nightmare. I'm living one.

And I can't tell anyone without getting into trouble or having it blabbed all over. That's why I'm writing it down. I can't avoid it anymore. Can't pretend it didn't happen. I have to get it out. All of it. Thank god Ms. Graham's off for a mental break. Our supply teacher is this old bald guy. He's letting us write for the whole period, as long as we sit quietly.

Okay. So anyway, here goes:

I get to the mall early Saturday to buy some stuff to bury the crap Mom made me pack in my knapsack for my supposed night at Katie's: a change of clothes, toiletries, a towel.

I do the mall tour, cramming my knapsack with brand names to impress Jason. (I plan to return them tomorrow, or guilt Dad into a cash advance. Once he hears I have a boyfriend, I figure he'll use that as an excuse to ditch our Sundays for more time with Brenda. Fine. Let him buy off his conscience.)

Last but not least, I pick up a fancy shopping bag for my new club gear: this wild, fluorescent pink-and-lime baby-doll number, plus a white Day-Glo boa and a cheap blonde beehive wig. When I add my sparkle makeup and orange eyelashes, Jason'll cream his jeans big time.

I look at my watch. It's 5:30. I grab a Coke and stake out Starbucks from a table behind a pillar at the opposite end of the food court. That way I'll be able to see Jason arrive without him thinking I've gotten there early. I can also check myself out in my compact.

I peek at the mirror every two minutes, making little makeup corrections, then wondering if the corrections are too much or too little, then smudging things, fixing smudges. It's unbelievable.

Pretty soon it's 6:00, then 6:05, then 6:10, then ohmigod 6:15! Panic attack! What if he came and I was staring at my compact and he didn't see me and left?

I start to sweat. I tell myself to stop; all sweating will do is wreck my makeup. That thought gets me even more flustered and I start to sweat all over again. Fanning my armpits just makes things worse. And now it's 6:25.

That's it—he's come and gone. He thinks I stood

him up. Or maybe he stood me up? Or he's at a different Starbucks? I'm soaking now, except for my throat, which is dry.

I glug my Coke. Somebody taps my shoulder from behind. I jump. Coke goes out my nose. I whirl around. It's him. I'm wiping my face with napkins and my make-up's ruined and he's laughing.

"It's not funny!"

"Sorry." He's still laughing.

"I thought we'd missed each other."

He points to the HMV store behind me. "I've been there the whole time."

"Why didn't you come over?"

"I was enjoying myself."

"Doing what?"

"Watching."

Jason's smiling, so I smile too, only I don't really get the joke.

"So ... what time's the movie?"

"There isn't going to be a movie," he says. "I've got a surprise."

The surprise is his folks are up at their cottage. His dad is this big-shot lawyer in something called Mergers and Acquisitions, and he just finished a major real estate deal. His parents decided to take off at the last minute, which means Jason has the house to himself. The idea of being alone with him gets me a little nervous. But also a little excited.

Next thing I know, he's got my stuff stashed on his motorcycle and I'm sitting behind him holding on like crazy. I've never been on a motorcycle before, and the wind in my face is scary and wonderful all at the same time. Plus the feel of my hands on his stomach makes my insides melt. I keep saying to myself, "Concentrate, Leslie. Concentrate or you could die"—not because I think we're going to crash or anything, but because I'm afraid I'm going to faint off his bike into traffic.

His house is in a really nice neighborhood, the kind with trees and a park, where everybody cuts their grass or has somebody cut it for them. There's a Camry in the driveway. I wonder if his folks have stayed home after all but he says no, it's his mom's. His parents always travel in his dad's BMW.

He parks beside the attached garage and helps me off. I have my knapsack on my back, but he carries the bag with my club stuff. Nobody's ever carried my things before, except for Katie the time I busted my collarbone.

When we get inside, I ask, "How come you go to our school when you live here?"

The answer's original, just like him. He went to a private school in Port Burdock, real snobby, and he was on all the teams. Everybody was after him because he was this big sports star, and it got to be too much. He tried to quit the teams, but they wouldn't let him because he was on an athletic scholarship. So he said, "Fine. I'm dropping out." And he did, just like that,

and came to our school, where nobody'd know him.
Amazing. I'd give anything to be popular. But he's got
the guts to just be himself.

Maybe he's so brave because he almost died. In grade
school, he got a major fever on a big family trip through
Asia. Getting well cost him a year, which is why he's
eighteen in grade twelve. But he made it. He cheated
death. I mean, he's a hero.

And rich. By the time he's showed me the upstairs,
it's clear his folks are loaded. The master bedroom has a
fireplace and a wall-size flat-screen TV, not to mention
walk-in closets and a six-piece en suite bathroom with a
sunken Jacuzzi.

For a second, I wonder if there's a reason we've ended
up here. Is he planning to make a move? I'm half scared
and half hoping, but he's a perfect gentleman. "That's
it," he says, and ushers me downstairs. I'm sort of disappointed, but also glad I can relax.

"Can I get you something to drink?" he asks as we
hit the kitchen.

"Sure. Do you have a Coke?"

His lip twitches in amusement. "Let me rephrase
that. Can I get you something to drink?"

My heart skips. I've never had a drink alone with a
guy before, and even if he can behave himself, I'm not
sure I can. All the same, I don't want to look stupid, and
one can't do any harm, can it? "What do you have?"

Instead of saying beer, wine, rum or whatever, he

starts reciting labels: "Johnnie Walker, Smirnoff, Gilbey's, Havana Club. Your wish is my command."

I decide to play it safe. "I'll have what you're having."

"Johnnie Walker on the rocks," he says, and takes a couple of tumblers out of the cupboard, shoots in a few cubes from the ice machine on the fridge and pours. I've never had scotch before; it's like I'm in the movies.

Jason hands me my drink and phones out for pizza while I have a sip. I almost choke. It's not like beer at all. I mean, it's puke foul. Who invented this stuff? All the same, if I don't finish it, I'll look like a reject. I know if I sip slowly I'll start retching, so I make a quick decision. I stop breathing and swallow it in two big gulps. It almost comes back up, but I focus on Jason's butt as he slouches at the counter by the telephone, and the sick feeling goes away.

Jason hangs up. He sees my empty glass. He's impressed. "You sure know how to knock it back."

"I was thirsty," I say.

"I better freshen that up, then," he says, pouring me another. Seeing as I've just made out I love the stuff, I can't very well say no.

We spend the next half hour drinking and talking about parents and teachers and kids at school, and I discover that scotch is a lot like swimming in the lake in May: it's okay once you get used to it.

Soon I'm on my fourth. It doesn't taste so bad anymore.

By the time Jason pours me my fifth, I'm telling him about Katie's sleepovers. He laughs, especially about the facials and fashion shows. I tell him how I hate Ashley and the others. He says I'm way out of their league. They're still kids, and I'm practically a woman. Coming from a senior who had his pick at Port Burdock, that's saying something.

When the pizza arrives, he says, "Let's eat down in the rec room."

I stand up. I fall back in my chair. "Whoa, what did they put in that scotch?"

"Scotch," he says, which for some reason we both find majorly funny.

"I think I better stick to beer."

He gets me a beer and we go down to his rec room, which is huge, with wood paneling and parquet everywhere. It's full of stuff—leather furniture and a pool table and a dart board and another flat-screen TV and a sound system. It's even got its very own minibar. Not to mention a bathroom. I go in and splash my face with cold water because I'm starting to feel a bit out of it.

I have a slight gap in my memory after that. We must have eaten the pizza, because I remember being back in the bathroom throwing up. I think the puking was after we smoked the joint, because that's when we decide we're too wasted to drive to a club and we'll just stay in his rec room. We start doing a little kissing. After all my worrying, kissing doesn't make me feel tense at all. It makes me feel great.

Then, just when I'm all relaxed, Jason starts to undo my pants. I say, "Maybe we should take a break." He says, "Why?" And I say, thinking fast, "So I can show you the stuff I bought at the mall." Jason gets this smile on his face and jokes how if I wasn't going to be doing a fashion show at Katie's, maybe I should do a fashion show for him. "Really?" I say. And he goes, "Yeah. I'd like that. Watching's fun."

Jason blasts hip hop out of the sound system, and suddenly I'm back in party mode. I go into the bathroom, change, and make my big entrance. Jason's turned the lights down and switched on this color wheel. Reds, greens and yellows swirl around the room. We're in our own private club.

Jason's on the couch. I prance up and down in front of him, twirling the Day-Glo boa. He's holding up his cell phone, making a video.

"Jason?"

"Keep going," he shouts over the music. "We'll watch it together. You're great!"

All of a sudden, I feel sexy. I'm, like, a professional dancer. I flirt for the cell. Wiggle around. Step backwards. Out of nowhere, I'm woozy. So woozy. I feel myself falling.

Next thing I know, I'm on the floor. The lights are still low, but the color wheel's off. The music too.

"Jason?"

He's gone. I'm alone. I'm cold. Cold? Oh my god, I'm naked! My clothes are all over the floor. Now, for the first time, I feel this soreness. This throbbing ache. Down there. There's blood and stuff caked on the inside of my legs.

What's going on? I can't remember.

I see his cell phone on a cushion. Oh no. It suddenly hits me. He was making a video.

I panic. Scramble over. Fumble with the buttons. Press play. There's me on the screen, dancing like an idiot. I see me fall. Hear him call my name. Then it stops. Thank god. He turned it off. Whatever happened, there's no record.

The lights go bright. Jason's in the doorway, yelling, "Get dressed. You gotta get out of here."

I squint. He's pulling my dress on. I try to say something. I can't. He wipes the floor with a towel and sprays air freshener. He hauls me up the stairs by my armpits.

He drops me at the landing. Runs back for my knapsack and shopping bag. Shoves twenty bucks in my hand. "I've called a cab to meet you at the end of the street. Go! Now!" He pushes me out the door, tosses my stuff after.

It's like a bad dream. I'm awake and asleep and I'm running down the street. I get to the corner. Slump on the curb. There's lights. A cab. I get inside.

It's two-thirty when it drops me off at my apartment building. I can't go upstairs; I'm supposed to be at Katie's. So I go down to the laundry room. It's got bright fluorescents, old machines, scuffed walls and cracked linoleum. At least I'll be alone.

There's a tub at the end of the machines. I strip down, wash myself, and dry off with my new top. Then I put on the clothes Mom made me pack for Katie's; they're in a plastic bag at the bottom of my knapsack. The new stuff I dump in a washer.

I'm not taking them home. I'm tying them in that plastic bag and tossing them in the garbage. But first I need them clean. I mean, what if somebody finds them? Sees the stains? It's like I've committed a crime.

And know the worst part? If I'd been awake and sober, I would have said yes.

Ten

After writing that down, I ran to the washroom. No way I wanted anyone to see me cry. I stayed in my cubicle till I figured everyone was gone for the day.

I figured wrong. As I walk down the hall, I see Katie, Ashley and a couple of other girls hanging around, pretending to be minding their own business. What they're really minding is the fancy envelope taped to my locker door.

I open it and take out the card. It's got a picture of a cartoon lion doing somersaults. Inside, it says, "You Drive Me Wild! No Lyin'!" Underneath is a handwritten note: "Had a great time Saturday. Hope you did too. I'm out on the bleachers catching a few rays. J."

The card. It's so casual—so *stupid*—it makes me think I imagined everything. Only I remember the blood, the pain. My face flushes: I'm mad. What planet is this guy on?

When I look up, the girls are staring at me. For one horrible second I think this is a repeat of a year ago, before my folks split, back in the time I was more or less normal.

I'd made the mistake of trying out for the junior cheerleading team. Needless to say, I didn't make it. Like—duh—to be a cheerleader you have to be cute and perky and able to do the splits without falling over. All the same, when the list went up on the phys ed bulletin board, I was crushed. While all the Cute and Perkies jumped up and down squealing, me and the other losers hung around like a bad smell, congratulating everyone and pretending to smile.

When I got to school the next day, there was a typed letter from Ms. Patrick, the cheerleading coach, stuck in the crack of my locker. It said how there'd been a mistake and my name should have been on the list and I should show up for the first practice that night after school.

I practically bounced off the walls all day. I told everybody, even phoned home and left a message for Mom and Dad. After school I was the first one into the changeroom.

But no sooner were we lined up on the track than Ms. Patrick hollered out, "Leslie Phillips, what are you doing here?"

"I came like you asked in the letter."

There were titters everywhere. Ms. Patrick said she'd like to speak to me in private and got Lara Babson, Queen of the Cute and Perkies, to lead warmup exercises while she walked me to her office. Everybody was staring. Katie, too, who'd come to cheer me on from the sidelines.

Inside, I showed Ms. Patrick the letter. She said I should've known it was fake since there was no handwritten signature. Also, that if there'd been a mistake she'd have mentioned it during morning announcements and added my name to the posted list along with her initials. She made it sound like the whole thing was my fault.

Then she asked who I thought could've done it. I just stared at the floor and shrugged. Who'd done it was the last thing on my mind. All I was thinking about was how I was going to explain to all the people I'd told that I wasn't on the team after all. That I was a sucker, a loser, a reject.

When I see the girls watching me read the card, these awful feelings come back. And I think, It's a set-up! They want to see me run to the bleachers so they can laugh at me!

But then Katie says, "Is it from him?" and my fears disappear. Katie would never hurt me like that. Here I was about to cry, and now all I want to do is laugh, because she's acting as excited as a new puppy meeting houseguests. I mean, I want to tell her not to wet the floor. Instead, I smile mysteriously and say, "Maybe." That gets the girls even more giddy. Except for Ashley, who looks like she just sucked a bug.

"What's he say?" Katie pants.

"Who cares?" snaps Ashley. "We have to hurry or we'll be late for choir practice."

Katie gives me one of her patented hand flaps and runs down the hall after Ms. A-Hole. At the corner she turns and calls back, "Phone me? Okay?"

"Whatever," I say, as if I have much more important things to do. Then I wink at the other girls, fan myself with my card and waltz down the corridor.

From the door leading to the track, I see him lounging on top of the bleachers. School's been out for a while now, but he's waited. It's like he knew I'd come.

There's no football practice today. Jason and I are alone except for one or two guys running laps. I walk across the field, climb halfway up the bleachers and stop. He must have heard me clunking on the boards but he keeps his eyes closed like he did the first day we met. Laid out in the sun, he looks sweet and innocent.

I'm scared. Not of *him*, exactly. It's just that, well, since Saturday I've been desperate to talk to him, but now that he's here I don't know what to say. So all I say is, "So."

He opens his eyes and flashes this slow easy smile. "What a perfect day."

I force myself not to look away. "I got your card."

"Good." There's a pause. He sits up, still smiling. "Where've you been?"

"Out of town with my folks. They took me to the cottage. Got your messages. Meant to call, e-mail. Sorry."

"That's okay." I stare at my feet.

He pats the bench beside him. "Come on up."

I stay where I am. "If you wanted to talk to me, how come you didn't meet me at my locker?"

He looks surprised. "Isn't it nicer to have some privacy? I mean, those friends of yours ..." He shakes his head like we've escaped from a bunch of baby sisters.

"Maybe it's nicer," I hesitate. Then I blurt out, "Or maybe you were scared I'd start yelling in front of them."

"Yelling?" He laughs. "What about?"

"You know." I hear my voice tremble so I shut up. I stare at his nose like I do with Mr. Manley. Only he doesn't have any nose hairs. He looks perfect. I feel confused.

Jason doesn't blink. His eyebrows scrunch up like he's puzzled, and I wonder—can he really not remember? Or have I made a mistake? Did nothing happen after all?

"Jason ..." I say in a voice so small I'm hardly breathing, "... did we?"

For a split second time stops, and for some bizarre reason I have a flash of driving with Dad when this bird swooped in front of the car and everything went into slow motion and I was praying the bird would escape and then *thump*. I hear Jason say, "Yeah." But the way he says it, it sounds like "So what?"

And I'm just standing there like a dummy with tears sliding off my face.

"Hey," Jason says. "Why the tears? It's not like you were a virgin or anything." He starts coming down like he wants to comfort me.

"Stay away." I wave my hands.

"But I don't get it," he says. "It was your idea."

Am I hearing this?

"I thought we should wait," he says. "You know, make it special. But you kept going, 'Now is special. Now.' Don't you remember?"

The truth is, I don't. But I would've remembered that.

"Leslie, you've gotta believe me." His voice is so sincere. "I'd never do anything to hurt you."

"Oh no? Well, what about the money? You made me feel like a hooker."

"Sorry. It's just, my folks got called back to town because Dad's deal was falling apart. It was after midnight. They phoned ahead to let me know they were coming, so I wouldn't think they were burglars or something."

I'm sniffling, but I'm listening.

"Leslie, please, you gotta remember. We wanted you to make a good first impression. But you were so wasted—we both were—we thought you should leave, come back to meet them another time. I paid for the cab, sure, but what was I supposed to do? You didn't have any money. I felt responsible. And I was way too drunk to drive."

I look in his eyes, and there's so much pain there it breaks my heart. How could I have thought those terrible things about him? I was zoned out of my mind, and he took care of me. I should be thanking him.

"Leslie, I have feelings for you. I mean it. If I've done or said anything to upset you, I'm sorry." He's all helpless now. How could I be so wrong?

"Did you mean it about meeting your folks?"

"Yeah. Unless you don't want to."

"No. That'd be fantastic."

He kisses me gently on the eyelids. "How about now?" he whispers.

I wash my face before heading out. I also change into the Mom-Approved Clothes stashed in my locker, in case Mrs. McCready has a thing against vinyl mini-skirts. They don't make me look like a nun exactly, but I'm decent enough not to scare anybody.

As it turns out, I'm not the one who needs to worry about looking decent. When we get to Jason's house, it's like Saturday: the Camry's in the drive but the BMW is missing. Jason says his dad must still be at work. Inside, the place is quiet as a tomb. I wonder if coming over was such a good idea. Then, from upstairs, I hear this voice. It sounds like a movie star, all husky and glamorous. "Is that you, Doug?"

"No, it's me, Mom."

"I am so annoyed with your father," the Voice exhales. It's coming down the stairs. "He promised he'd be home early. We're supposed to be at the Richardsons' in an hour and he hasn't phoned."

Now I see the Voice, and It sees me. I'm not sure who's more surprised.

Mrs. McCready could be a model. She's tall with a long neck, designer hair and an amazing figure. But there's something wrong with the picture. She's in her slip, with a mud mask on her face and a glass of tomato juice in her hand.

"This is Leslie. Leslie, this is my mom."

Mrs. McCready decides to pretend everything's normal. "How do you do?" she nods, then tilts her chin at Jason. "You didn't mention we'd be having company. Your father and I are going out."

"We're working on a geography project for school tomorrow. We'll be down in the rec room."

She considers this briefly. "Good. There's pie in the fridge if you get hungry."

Before I know it, Jason and I are heading downstairs.

"Does your mom really think we're in the same grade?" I whisper.

"My mom doesn't think at all after three o'clock." He winks. I don't get it. "Leslie, wake up. You think that's just tomato juice she's drinking?"

"But she acts so sober."

"Practice makes perfect." He puts his arms around me. "Speaking of practice ..."

I resist, but the kiss is so nice I start kissing him back. My eyes are closed, and there's little flashes of light. It feels like that first day on the football field, only better.

After a few minutes, Jason breaks away. He goes into the bathroom and brings back a towel, folding it carefully in the middle of the sofa.

"What's that for?"

"You're my girlfriend, aren't you?"

His girlfriend? Wow! "Yeah, I guess so."

"Well ..." He flashes that smile and sweeps his arm towards the sofa as if he's a waiter directing me to the best table in some fancy restaurant. "It's not like we haven't before."

That's true. I mean, the damage is already done, and if we're going out, well ... All the same, I feel weird. "Your mom's upstairs."

"So we'll keep quiet. Besides, she only hears what she wants to hear. Hey, if it'll make you feel any better ..." He puts on some music.

"What if she comes down?"

"She won't. She doesn't like surprises." I'm still not sure about things, but I melt when he looks in my eyes and whispers, "I love you, you know."

Somehow we end up on the sofa, and then, well, things go so fast I hardly know it's happened, except I hurt. We're even still dressed, except for my panties are around my knees and my sweater's pulled up. All of a sudden I want to get out of there. How can I be so in love and feel like shit?

"I should go. My mom'll be expecting me."

"Sure." He nods, as if he's secretly happy. "I'll drive you back."

Mrs. McCready is posed at the picture window in the living room, dressed in something out of *Vogue*. She's still holding her tomato juice. "Finished your project?"

"Yeah."

"You must be a good influence on him," she says to me. Her eyelid twitches.

It's six-thirty by the time I get home. There's salad and a plate of cold macaroni and cheese waiting for me on the kitchen table. My mom is waiting too.

"Where were you?" she asks.

"Over at Katie's."

"Is that so."

From the tone of her voice, I'm not sticking around to chat. I head down the hall to my room, calling back, "Yeah. We were working on a project for school tomorrow. You have a problem with that?"

Mom follows me. "Yes, I have a problem with that," she fires back. "If you were at Katie's, perhaps you'd like to explain why she called from choir practice asking you to phone her about a card you received."

"It's none of your business."

"As long as you live here, everything is my business."

"Yeah, right." And I slam the door in her face.

Eleven

One of Mom's favorite expressions is "Let sleeping dogs lie." She says this all the time when I ask her about Dad and other women: "Leslie, just let sleeping dogs lie."

I joke, "Does that mean I should let Dad lie, on account of he's a sleeping dog?"

She gives me a dirty look. "I mean, don't bring up unpleasantness from the past. Okay?"

Fine, so Mom doesn't have a sense of humor. But at least you'd think she'd practice what she preaches. Isn't it her job to set an example? I figured a good night's sleep and she'd drop the whole cop routine about where I was last night. But no. Seven o'clock her alarm goes off, and she's still on my case.

Well, if she's going to be a busybody, I'm going to be a bitch.

"For the last time, Leslie, where were you?"

"Wherever will make you happy."

Pretty soon it's eight, and she's so wired from her coffee and my crap she's running in circles like a hamster on speed. I'm eating bran flakes while she screams at me from the bathroom—brushing her teeth with one hand, spraying deodorant with the other—when somebody buzzes from the lobby.

"Will you see who it is?"

"I'm having breakfast."

"Leslie, I'm late enough for work as it is."

Whoever's in the lobby buzzes again. Mom runs out of the bathroom, toothpaste drooling off her chin. "Yes?" she hollers into the intercom. She mouths at me: "You're grounded."

"Annabelle Florists," says this voice.

Mom looks surprised. So do I. "Come on up."

The delivery guy arrives in no time. He hands her a bundle done up in fancy wrapping paper. Inside, there's a dozen long-stemmed red roses and a note. Mom reads: "Leslie. Thanks for a great geography lesson. J."

She passes me the roses. I'm in another world. I cradle the bouquet like it's a baby.

Mom's not impressed. "I take it he's where you were last night."

"Somebody's just sent me roses for the first time in my life. Can't you be happy?"

"Does 'somebody' have a name?" She wipes the toothpaste off her mouth.

"Why do you always have to spoil everything?" Instead of fighting, I want to cry. I sink into my chair and bury my head so she won't see.

"Pooky Bear ..."

"Don't call me that."

"I'm sorry."

I feel her hand on my shoulder and shake it off.

"Look, I'm happy for you. I just don't like you sneaking around behind my back."

I wait till I'm sure my voice won't break. "His name is Jason McCready."

"Have you been seeing him for a long time?"

"Who says I've been seeing him?"

Mom takes a deep breath, smoothes her clothes and sets a stool under the cupboard over the stove. "Why don't I get the vase and we put those flowers in some water?"

"You're going to be late for work."

"This is more important."

Out comes my great-grandmother's crystal vase and we're cutting the ends of the stems with a kitchen knife, arranging the roses, starting to have a good time, even. Half of me feels wonderful, and the other half wants to gag.

"They're beautiful." Mom smiles.

"Yeah." I want to shut up now, but I have this sudden, overwhelming need to say his name. "Jason's great. The other girls are really jealous." Saying his name out loud felt good. So good, I forget Mom only acts nice when she wants something. She doesn't let me forget for long.

"Why don't you invite him over?"

Thunk. "Here?"

"What's the matter with here?"

"Mother, please. Are you trying to humiliate me?"

"I beg your pardon?"

I roll my eyes. And—bang—it's like the last five minutes never existed.

"Don't tell me you're ashamed of your own home," Mom says.

"Aren't you?"

Mom kind of slumps. She puts the stool away, folds the fancy wrapping paper and drops the stem ends in the garbage. I feel horrible.

"It's nothing personal, Mom," I say. "It's just, well, Jason's parents are important, like his dad does big business deals and everything, and they live in this enormous house and everything's new and expensive."

She gives me her Mom-on-a-Cross face. "You know, Leslie, it takes more than money to make a home."

Pass me the barf bag. "I never said a home is only money," I shoot back. "A home's also supposed to be a place where people love each other. But I don't see a lot of that around here either."

I want Mom to say something. I want her to yell at me, even. But she doesn't. She just puts her coat on slowly and heads out to work.

Twelve

When I get to school, Jason's at my locker waiting for me. Leaning on the lockers opposite mine, actually, in his leather jacket and shades. It's like he's sunning himself indoors.

"Thanks for the roses," I say, loud enough for everyone to hear.

He drapes over me, his hands on my bum, and gives me a kiss. I feel self-conscious but also proud: the girls will know we're together.

"Came to walk you to class. Get your stuff. We'll be late."

Everyone's looking at us, and my head bobs like one of Aunt Betty's knick-knack china Dutch girls. I can't help myself. I scramble my books out of my locker with a wink at Katie. Then, without looking where I'm going, I bump right into him.

"Hey, if it isn't the Leslie doll," he laughs. "Wind her up, she walks into a wall." I hear a few titters and just about die, but not for long. In one smooth move, he slides his arm across my shoulder. I put my free hand into his back pocket—up yours, Ashley—and together we float off to class.

We're together at lunch, too, just us on the bleachers. I tell him about the grilling I got from Mom, and how he's lucky to have a mother who minds her own business.

Jason cocks his head. "Actually, I think meeting your mom is a good idea."

"What?"

"It'll help keep her onside."

Onside. How did Jason get so smart at psychology?

But he has more surprises. First, he asks if I'd like to see Pigjam next Friday.

"Aren't they sold out?"

"No sweat, I got contacts. The show's at eight, I'll pick you up around seven. That way I can meet your mom and we'll have an excuse to split quick."

"You're brilliant!"

Then the best surprise of all. He reaches into his knapsack and pulls out a box, all gift-wrapped. "For you," he smiles.

Inside is a brand-new cell phone, just like his. It can take photos and videos, and I can program a different ring depending on who's calling. Plus it lets me online to text. There's even a GPS chip so if I want to find out how to get someplace, I just type in the address and a map pops up with a route for how to get there. I mean, this cell does everything but homework.

I want it so bad, but I hand it back. "I can't afford to pay the bills."

He laughs. "Don't worry. I'll look after it."

"Jason, no. It's too much."

"Nothing's too much for you. Or what I want to do for you." His eyes go soulful. "See, Leslie, it's about your mom. I'm sure she's great and all. But she's also a wacked-out control freak. You've basically said so yourself. With this cell, you can contact whoever you want, whenever you want, without her looking over your shoulder. Take it. Please. It's not just a cell. It's freedom."

I start to hug him like crazy, but there's this voice calling from across the football field: "Leslie!" It's Katie. She and the gang are on their way back from Mister Pizza's. While the rest of the girls go into the school, she runs over with this goofy grin on her face.

I send her these very strong Stay-Away-Katie vibes. But apparently the only messages Katie picks up come from God or something, because she sure doesn't get mine. She comes right up, like I'm supposed to welcome her into our private conversation. I don't.

"Yeah?"

"I thought I'd come over and say hi." She gives a girlie finger wave to Jason. "I've seen you around, but we've never been actually introduced. You must be Jason."

"And who must you be?" he says, polite and sarcastic all at once.

"Katie. I've heard so much about you."

"And I've heard so much about you."

"Really?" Katie's face lights up like she's in kinder-garten and the teacher's put a big gold star on her forehead.

Wake up, Katie, I think. He's insulting you. Don't

you get it? Why don't you leave us alone? But it's too late. Jason's getting ready to leave.

"I'd love to stay, shoot the breeze," he says, "but I've got things to do." I go to follow him, but he holds up his hand. "You stay with your pal Katie here. I'll catch you later." He walks off without looking back.

Katie's all moon-eyed. You'd think she just talked to a movie star or something. But me, I'm heartsick. Jason and I were having such a good time, and she went and scared him away. A wave of anger surges inside me. But just as I'm about to let rip, Katie stammers, "So, are you guys doing it?"

My heart skips. "Who says we're doing it?"

Katie looks at my face and gasps. "Oh no, you are!"

"I never said that!" I shout. "I asked you, 'Who says?'"

"Nobody."

"*Nobody?*"

"Okay. Ashley. She says that's why Jason's started to hang around."

"What a bitch."

"Well, are you?"

"If Jason and I were doing it, do you think I'd tell you?"

"Yeah. Why not?"

"You can't keep your mouth shut, that's why not."

"Are you still mad I told Ashley you made up boy-friends?"

"Among other things," I say.

"What other things?"

"Last night you told my mom you were at choir practice. I told her I was at your place. You got me in so much trouble—"

"It's not my fault you lied to your mother."

"And it's not my fault you're a moron."

Katie's eyes fill. "Leslie, why are you yelling at me? What's the matter? We used to be friends."

"Used-to-be's right, isn't it? And I suppose that's my fault. All I know is I used to have a friend I could count on, but now she only has time for my worst enemy. Well, I don't care. I have a boyfriend who loves me and I don't need to waste my time with a nerdy little baby who needs her mommy's permission to pee."

Katie's face disintegrates. I watch as she turns and runs across the grass, shoulders heaving.

Serves her right. I've never let anyone come between us—not parents, not friends, nobody. So how come she's the one acting hurt? All the same, I feel like a turd.

By the time I get to math class, I'm not mad anymore. While Mr. Kogawa writes math equations on the board, I scribble a note and slip it on Katie's desk. It says, "I'm so sorry. You'll always be my best friend, no matter what." There's a little pause, and then Katie turns around with a look so serious I don't know whether to laugh or cry. She whispers, "Me too," and I know which: I cry.

Thirteen

Even after I made up with Katie, I was still worried that she might have wrecked things with Jason. I had this bizarre panic that when he walked away from the bleachers, he wasn't going to catch me later, that he'd left me with the cell and taken off for good.

One of the awful things about dating guys is, out of the blue, for no reason, they can just stop calling you. One minute you're their girlfriend, the next minute you're not. And they won't even say why. It's like they're afraid to face you and have you get mad at them. So there's always this scary feeling in the back of your mind. At the same time they're smiling and laughing with you, they may be planning to split. I know I'm talking like a sudden expert and all. But you don't have to watch a talk show to prove what I'm saying—just ask any girl in my school.

But Jason's different. Not only did he catch me later, he was at my locker after class.

We went and studied at his place. (Well, okay, we didn't really study.) And ever since, well, he's been after me 24/7. I get nonstop texts. Stuff like, "HOW R U?" or "S'UP?" or "U WEARING PANTYS 2DAY?" First time I got the last one, I blushed, but I have to admit it made me feel sexy.

He wants to see me every night, too. Says he's afraid

to let me out of his sight. Romantic or what? He's meeting me after school today and tomorrow, and then it's Friday and the Pigjam concert.

As for Mom, Jason's psychology trick worked great. I told her he wanted to meet her this weekend, and she chilled right out. She said if I wanted to study at his place she'd hold supper for me—"I'm glad you're finally doing some homework!"—as long as I was back by seven and his mom was home.

"Deal," I said. "Oh, and before he comes, will you help me tidy the place up?"

As soon as I said that she got this amused grown-up look.

"What's so funny?"

"If you want to tidy up, he must be very special."

I hate it when Mom does that. It's like I'm a baby or something, this cute little pet put on earth to entertain her. It was especially annoying this time, because she was getting even for all the times I've been a slob. Last year she kept complaining my room was a pigsty. I told her if it bothered her so much she should stop looking at it, and got my "Keep Out" sign.

But who cares? Mom can have her little joke if it keeps her from asking questions. Let's face it, if she knew the truth about me and Jason, she'd have a heart attack. Maybe even die.

Just thinking about Mom being dead makes me freak. Dad might as well be worm meat; he's out of my life these days. If Mom was gone too, I don't know what I'd do. Sometimes I imagine myself screaming my lungs inside out or throwing myself out a window or stabbing myself to death with scissors.

Seriously, the idea that Mom could die because of something I did drives me crazy. It's what I'm thinking about when I step into English today. And—speaking of nervous breakdowns and going crazy—guess who's back? Ms. Graham. She's smiling like a maniac. If she doesn't watch out, her cheeks are going to explode.

The class is so shocked we don't even talk, much less get rowdy. I mean, eyeballs are hanging out of their sockets, and we just sort of drop into our seats and stare at her, as if she's a mirage or something.

"It's great to be back," she says. "I've missed you and I'm feeling much better, thanks, and I know the rest of the year is going to be really special."

They better adjust her medication. Still, the tremor in her hands is mostly gone, and she's hardly sweating at all. That is, until she asks how many of us filled out our *To Kill a Mockingbird* question and answer sheets. We look at her all innocent, like we haven't a clue what she's talking about.

"You mean while I've been gone you haven't done anything? Why, every day you were to read twenty pages and answer a sheet of questions. I left instructions!"

Was she born simple, or does she work at it? The average supply teacher has a hard time figuring out how to turn on a TV. You think they can follow instructions? And when it's a regular teacher supervising, why should they care? They have a million students of their own to worry about.

Ms. Graham starts rummaging around in her filing cabinet, still smiling but definitely getting twitchy. "The handouts were right here. Oh dear." And now it looks like she's having a near-death experience because guess what? The Handouts Are Missing! Her eyes do that gerbil thing, and you can see her trying to figure out what's happened. Did she actually forget to make them? Is her memory of them a hallucination? Or maybe one of the janitors broke in and stole them?

Naturally, the handouts aren't missing at all. The truth is, aside from a couple of goofs, the supply teachers gave them to us. They just didn't get done is all. But we never did them when she was here, so why would we start when she was away? Ms. Graham is too good-hearted. She gives our class credit for giving a shit. Has she really forgotten what we're like?

While she was away, the guys at the back played cards as always, and the rest of us either caught up on our other homework or stared out the window or wrote in our journals. I also read the book, but only because I wanted to. (It would be nice to have a dad like Atticus instead of the loser I got stuck with. I mean, I can't even imagine Atticus trading his daughter for a skank like Brenda.)

Anyway, things with Ms. Graham are getting really

interesting when Cindy Williams puts up her hand. "Are these the handouts, Ms. Graham?" she asks, all dimples and curls. She holds up a binder full of neatly completed question and answer sheets. (Cindy gets straight As, and she writes with big fat letters and signs her name with a little heart over the *i*. She makes me gag.)

"So you did get the handouts!" Ms. Graham exclaims, and she's back on her spaceship to Planet Happy. "Good, good." She hops to her desk. "That means you're all prepared for a little content quiz."

Before you can say "Boo Radley," Ms. Graham's handed out this test full of multiple choices and fill-in-the-blanks. It takes about two minutes, and then she collects them and gives us our journals. We're supposed to write while she marks.

We don't write very long before Ms. Graham calls us to attention. It seems only four or five people have bothered to read the book. Most of the content quizzes are either blank or have supposedly funny comments written in where the answers should go. Such as: "Jem reads <u>porno</u> to dead gophers."

That one's courtesy of Nicky Wicks. Ms. Graham reads it out loud to make him look stupid. But instead, the card players hoot "Aw right!" and Nicky bows as if he's a hero or something.

Ms. Graham's losing it. "There are only two of you mature enough to call yourselves grade ten students," she yells. "Cindy Williams and Leslie Phillips. Because they did their work, they each received a perfect score. I trust the rest of you will learn from their example."

Waydego, Ms. Graham. I mean, can I die now?

Then the biggest unfairness of all. She announces she's going to give everyone a second chance, and she tosses the tests in the recycling bin. Unbelievable. She goes and humiliates me, and the test isn't even going to count!

To make sure everyone is prepared for the makeup test, she says we're going to read the book aloud, up and down the aisles, half a page each from start to finish. The only good thing is, because Cindy and I read it, we get to write in our journals instead. So for the next ten years while everyone's mumbling their way through *To Kill a Mockingbird*, I get to text Jason, think about after-school "studying" and count the days to Friday, which is what I'm doing now.

Fourteen

Friday arrived like magic. Jason buzzed up at seven. I let him in and hey, was he ever a knockout: tanned, gelled and manicured, in a black embroidered shirt, brushed cotton pants and shoes to die for.

"Parents love it when the guy's well dressed and punctual," he'd told me. Well, not Mom. When things are perfect, she gets suspicious.

I make the introductions.

"Pleased to meet you, Jason," Mom nods. She acts polite, the sort of polite that's almost rude.

Jason ignores the attitude. "Pleasure's mine, Mrs. Phillips," he says, shaking her hand. He sounds way mature, like he sells imported cars or something.

"Leslie tells me you're going to the Pigjam concert. What kind of a band is Pigjam?" Translation: "There better not be drugs."

But Jason's a mind reader. "Pretty mainstream," he replies. "I don't go for rap or hip hop."

"Good. That sounds like fun, then."

"I hope so. The tickets are a fortune. Luckily, Dad managed to get us comps through a client of his."

Is Mom impressed? No way. "That's nice," she says, like it's no big deal. What's up her butt now?

Jason looks at me, still smiling. "Is that all you're wearing?"

I'm not dressed slutty or anything, but I've only put on enough to pass inspection. I wonder what he's up to, and then it clicks: he's out to impress Mom. I laugh and come back in these designer jeans and a fancy-knit sweater. "We gotta go, Mom, or we'll be late."

Jason opens the door for me. "There's no need to wait up, Mrs. Phillips. Your daughter's in good hands."

"Actually, Jason," Mom says tightly, "Leslie's well-being is in my hands."

"Absolutely," Jason agrees without missing a beat.

Can he keep his cool or what. He shakes her hand again, and we're out the door.

Jason's got his mom's Camry. We get to the stadium's underground garage and back into a parking space against the far wall between two empty cars. I get out and head for the elevator, but Jason's fiddling with something.

"Hurry up, we'll be late."

"Relax. The opening act'll take an hour."

And now I see what he's doing. He's folded out one of those cardboard sunscreens and put it across the front windshield. He opens the door to the backseat.

"Jason! Not here!"

"No, something else, dummy," he says. "I've got something for you."

"Can't you give it to me out here?"

But I get in the backseat anyway and Jason pulls out a joint. "Grade A. No kidding. I got it off a special friend."

"What if we get busted?"

"Nobody checks third-basement parking. Besides, we're at the end, cars on either side, a screen up. Come on, you're acting like that Katie geek."

We have the joint, but I don't get the giggles. I'm too paranoid. Especially when he puts his hand up my sweater. I knew this was going to happen.

"Jason, you said we wouldn't. I mean, we're in public!"

"It'll be exciting. Trust me."

As if.

Jason has me back home at five minutes before twelve. He doesn't come in.

As usual Mom's waiting up, only instead of sitting at the kitchen table, she's in the living room with her back to me, watching some old movie.

It's creepy. She doesn't say a word. There's just this low sound of voices coming from the TV and her sitting absolutely still.

For a minute, I think maybe she's fallen asleep. That'd be perfect. Because I don't want to get close to her before having a shower.

But just as I reach the door of the bathroom, she says in a loud voice, "How was the concert?"

"Fine," I say. I'm trying to sound cheerful, but my throat is tight. Before she has a chance to say anything else, I scoot inside and close the door.

Mom's still waiting for me when I come out wrapped in a towel. She's turned the TV off and is sitting at the table. "Leslie, could I speak to you for a minute?" She's not mad. She sounds strange, like I better say yes or there's really going to be trouble.

"Okay," I say. "Just let me put something on."

I come back in track pants and a top.

Mom sits quietly for a minute and then says: "Leslie, how old is Jason?"

"Eighteen."

"Don't you think it would be better if you dated someone more your own age?"

"What, I'm a baby or something? Or he's this old-man-pervert child molester?"

"No."

"Then what?"

Mom looks at me very seriously. "Honey, I don't know how to put this ..."

"Don't bother. I knew you wouldn't like him. I mean, if God asked me for a date you'd find something to complain about. Jason's here on time, he's dressed up, he opens the door for me, he has a nice family and I'm back before twelve. What more do you want?"

"It's only that—"

"Never mind. You don't want me to be happy!"

"No. No. Of course I want you to be happy. It's just ... I don't want you to get hurt."

I want to say something smart. But I don't. Instead, before I can stop myself, I give her a big hug. She holds me tight. I feel like a baby, but all of a sudden I don't care.

Fifteen

I've been skipping Ms. Graham's class big time. For the last couple of weeks I've shown up for attendance, then asked to go to the bathroom and haven't come back. Jason has a spare last period, so we've been taking off to his place to "study."

Today, though, I got narced out by Mr. Manley in the parking lot. He made me get off Jason's motorcycle and marched me back to class. "This isn't the first time you've roared off early, is it?" he demanded.

"Oh no? Prove it."

Since Ms. Graham always has me marked present, he can't do anything. But to make sure I don't leave early again, he wants me to report to the office at the end of the day for the next two weeks. Otherwise, he's calling home.

Normally, I wouldn't care. But Mom's not stupid. It used to be she'd grill me about boys that didn't exist, but that was because she wanted to be reassured. Lately, she hasn't been asking much of anything. It's as if she suspects what we're up to but is too afraid to know. All the same, if she hears I'm cutting class with Jason, for sure she'll want a "talk" and after that she won't be able to pretend anymore. Poor Mom. I can't imagine it. If she finds out I'm having sex *officially* I'll die.

Not that Jason would care.

No, forget I said that. That's Katie talking. Jason does care; I know he does. He loves me. I mean, he writes me poems, texts me kisses, and everything. And he's always giving me presents, little surprises like this pinkie ring and a charm bracelet with a big silver J on it. He says the J is a symbol that he's my lucky charm. Sweet or what? Katie should shut her mouth. What does she know about guys anyway?

Still, I wish Jason didn't make such a big deal about sex. He brings it up all the time. Like, he tells me to keep my cell on hum, so he can vibrate in my pants. And when we're together—why do we *always* have to do it? If I tell him I don't want to, he gets all mad. "What's the matter? You frigid? A lesbian, maybe?"

"No," I say. "It's just—couldn't we see a movie instead? This once?" Then he says how I don't love him, and how much he loves me, and how much he needs me, and he keeps going on and on until finally I say, "Okay, I'm sorry. Forget I said anything."

The good news is, despite all the sex I'm not pregnant.

For the first little while, I kept telling myself that each time was going to be the last. But then we'd get together and one thing always led to another. Finally, this one day, I gave up lying to myself and checked Wikipedia about menstrual cycles.

Talk about scary. I'm pretty good at math, and counting the days since my last period, I started imagining symptoms like crazy. At lunch, I ran out and got one of those tests from the pharmacy. I sat in my bathroom cubicle on the second floor and waited to see if the thingy'd turn color. Was I ever relieved!

That afternoon I told Jason we'd been lucky, but I'm at my peak and maybe he should use a condom.

He acted shocked. "You mean you're not taking care of that?"

"I can't go to my doctor. I'm too embarrassed.

Anyway, a condom's good for other things, too. You know, AIDS, STDs."

"Are you accusing me of something?"

"No."

"Good. So relax. I'm fine."

But now I'm curious. "Have you been tested?"

"No."

"Then how do you know you're fine?"

"I know." His fists clenched.

I tried to calm him down. "Look, I believe you. Sorry. But we can't take chances. I'm only fifteen. If I get pregnant, they're going to want to know who did it."

"Who says they'd ever have to know you were pregnant? You'd just have to see somebody. My dad knows people." I must've looked hurt because he got all sulky. "Fine. Be that way," he said, and fished out a condom, like I was really inconveniencing him or something.

When he's in one of those moods, I've learned not to mouth off. I just look at the floor and whisper, "Using a condom doesn't make that much difference, does it?"

Then he gets all tender. He strokes my hair, cups my head in his hands and kisses me gently on the forehead. "It's just that I want to be closer to you."

I feel so guilty. "Me too," I say and kiss him back. "I'll figure something out."

What I figure out is, I can steal pills from Mom for a couple of months. Sneaking them won't be a problem. Mom had almost a year's supply when Dad left and she hasn't used them since. They're at the back of a drawer beside the sink in the bathroom. She's probably forgotten about them, for all I know. For sure she won't remember how many she had. So that's what I've been doing.

Taking the pill makes me less paranoid, but I'm still uncomfortable with the sex bit.

At the beginning, I worried his mom would catch us. I'd be like, "Jason, Jason please don't," and he'd be laughing, "Please don't what? Please don't stop?" As it turns out, though, he was right about her. She goes through so much "tomato juice" I hardly think she'd notice if she waltzed right in and sat down beside us.

What gets me is actually "doing it." The kissing part is fine, but that only lasts a minute, and then he's on top of me and I can't even move. I can hardly breathe. A few times I tried to stop him, but I ended up with bruises, and once my blouse got ripped, which took a lot of explaining to Mom.

"I was climbing over a fence at school and it got caught."

"What were you doing climbing over a fence?"

"What do you care?"

"Answer the question."

"Okay, I wasn't climbing over a fence." I rolled my eyes, all sarcastic. "Jason wanted to have sex and he ripped my clothes off. Happy?"

"That isn't funny," Mom said and dropped the subject.

It's amazing, but sometimes if you tell the truth, people will act as though it's a lie.

I guess it's not that bad. At least it's quick. I'm like, "Ow ow ow ow ow," and then Jason groans like he's constipated and says, "That was great," and I go, "Yeah," to keep him happy.

One time I guess I wasn't enthusiastic enough. "All you can say is 'Yeah'?"

That pissed me off. Before I could stop myself, I went, "What do you want? You want me to turn into the school marching band? Do a production number? Light up some fireworks, maybe? Blow the roof off?"

He slapped me.

"What was that for?"

"Watch your lip."

That's why I like it better when we get stoned first. Getting stoned doesn't make me paranoid anymore. It lets me zone out. I can stare at a point on the ceiling, or the roof of the car, and pretend I'm not there till it's over.

Why am I always complaining? Why am I such a bitch? Jason loves me, I know it, he says so. Why am I always so negative? I should think of the good stuff— riding on his motorcycle, my charm bracelet.

The other girls tell me how lucky I am. Except for Ashley. Last week, as per usual, she said juniors who date seniors are sex toys, like I'm a slut or something.

"You'd go out with Jason in a flash," I said. "Except he'd never ask you."

"Oh please," she sniffed. "I'm not boy-crazy like you."

"Bullshit," I snapped. "The only reason you're a virgin is because you've never had a date."

"Well, the only reason you're not pregnant is because you're lucky."

"Liar."

"Skank."

I pushed her.

"Girls." It was Mr. Manley. "Is there a problem?"

"No, sir," Ashley said.

"Then get to class. Leslie, I'd like a word with you in my office."

What else is new? I glanced at Katie. She was looking at the floor; you'd think someone had died. My insides heaved.

Why does everything go wrong? Why am I such a failure?

Right now I'm looking at Ms. Graham. I'll bet she asks the same things. I wonder if she's ever been in love. I wonder if she's lonely. I wonder if maybe being lonely is better. All I know is, since falling in love with Jason I've been the loneliest of all.

Sixteen

Ms. Graham's gone berserk, and it's only the end of October. Nicky Wicks is lucky he's alive. Mr. Manley is supervising us right now, and for the first time in history, this room is quiet as a morgue.

The class started out pretty ordinary—a lot of bad readers and paper airplanes. We were at the part in the book where Tom is about to get lynched and Scout has the guts to stand up in front of the whole mob—and she's way younger than me!

Anyway, Ms. Graham was going on about how this was one of her favorite scenes, and if everybody would just settle down and listen they'd really enjoy it. Her face was alive, like she meant it, like it mattered—and all of a sudden I got this flash of why she wanted to be a teacher. She actually cares about this stuff.

When I think that, I feel really bad. Caring about something so much it hurts and having everybody laugh at you—talk about brutal. I pictured Ms. Graham as a teenager with her nose in some book, and the whole school teasing her and being mean. Well, it's thirty years later and nothing's changed. How does she get out of bed in the morning?

My head filled with this crazy idea that I should stand on my desk and yell at everyone to shut up. Of course I didn't. I'm not suicidal. But I had the idea.

As per usual, Nicky Wicks was the ringleader. He's discovered he can make himself cross-eyed by touching his tongue to his nose, and he kept turning around to show the card players at the back, who found it majorly hilarious.

"Nicky!" Ms. Graham said. Nicky stopped. Two seconds later he was doing it again. "Nicky!!" Nicky stopped. Two seconds later, the same thing. "Nicky!!!" This went on until nobody was paying any attention to Ms. Graham's favorite scene at all. They were just laughing at Nicky, who was basically daring her to do something.

She did.

Out of the blue, she wheeled to the blackboard, grabbed a yardstick, charged at Nicky and smashed it down. He leaned back just in time. The yardstick broke across his desk. Everyone froze. She could have cracked his head open.

Ms. Graham went white as chalk. The end of the yardstick fell out of her hand. She teetered there looking around the room at the silent faces. It was as if she wasn't sure where she was or what had happened. And then this tear slid down her cheek and onto her neck. She didn't say anything, just turned and wobbled out of the room slowly, like a robot.

Things stayed quiet for a long time. Then someone whispered, "Are you all right?" to Nicky. He nodded. In a few minutes, the talking was wild. Mr. Manley came in, and everything went silent again. He glared at us:

"Get to work, people." Everyone opened their binders and kept their heads down.

Poor Ms. Graham. She didn't mean to lose it. If you ask me, it's a miracle she hasn't attacked someone before. Also a miracle that Nicky's brains aren't splattered all over the ceiling. If they were, there'd have been TV crews all over the place, and her picture would have been plastered everywhere. Now this'll all be forgotten, except by our class. And Ms. Graham. I bet it haunts her till the day she dies.

"There but for the grace of God go I." Katie's started to say that a lot. It's weird hearing it come from somebody under forty, but Katie says she doesn't care. Her church told her it's good to say it when you see somebody homeless or really sick. From now on I'm going to say it whenever I think of Ms. Graham.

Seventeen

Things happening with or without a reason, things we regret—maybe that's why old people lose their minds. Their heads get too full of things they'd rather forget.

I know mine will. It's packed already. There are so many things I've done that make me ashamed. Like never standing up for Ms. Graham. She may be a lousy teacher, but she tries. And how have I thanked her? By bad-mouthing her behind her back and sleeping in the middle of her lessons.

Mom wouldn't do that. She sticks up for people. I remember buying groceries with her a couple of years back. At the checkout counter, there was a little boy ahead of us with his mother. He took a candy bar from the lowest rack by the cash register. His mother yelled, and he cried, and she started hitting him.

Mom said in a loud voice, "Stop it! What do you think you're doing?" The woman said it was none of Mom's business. Mom said, "Children being hit is everyone's business." The whole line was staring at us. I was so embarrassed. But the woman stopped beating on her kid, and afterwards I was proud of Mom for doing it.

That's another thing I feel ashamed about: being so horrible to Mom. I love her. But I sure don't act like I do. I slam my door in her face. I rub it in about Dad leaving. Sometimes I feel like I'm mean to everybody who cares about me.

I was worrying about all this when Katie came up to me before school. It's like she has mental telepathy or something.

"I've been thinking over what you said a few weeks back, out by the bleachers," she goes, all serious.

"Katie, please. I didn't mean it."

"No. You're right. I've been so wrapped up in things I've ignored you. I'm sorry."

I don't know what to say, so I nod.

"Anyway," she continues, "I have to get some new tops and I wondered if maybe you want to go shopping with me."

"When?"

"I don't know. Some day after school."

I hesitate. What would I say to Jason? If I don't see him every day, he gets in one of his moods. Then I remember he has a dentist appointment tomorrow. "What about tomorrow afternoon?"

"I have choir practice."

"Oh, right."

I guess I look disappointed, because Katie takes a deep breath. "Okay. Tomorrow. Missing one practice won't hurt."

I'm amazed. For Katie, missing choir is almost worse than murder. I'm even more amazed next day when Ashley lays on this guilt trip and Katie says, "Look, Ashley, God's hardly going to strike me dead or anything."

Our trip starts out great: we're playing spy up and down the mall, laughing at all the sales clerks who go on Red Alert when they see a teenager come near their store. We put on accents, pretending to be rich people. It's pretty stupid, but it gives us the giggles all the same.

The fun stops when we start trying on tops. Lots of girls are embarrassed about getting undressed—after gym, some even change with a towel wrapped around them—but me and Katie have seen each other naked so many times we don't care. So anyway, we're squashed together in this tiny changeroom tossing stuff on and off when all of a sudden Katie goes, "Oh my god! What's that on your back?"

I get really scared. I imagine I have this malignant growth or something. But when I look in the mirror, all I see is a bruise. It's not hurting. I'd even forgotten I had it.

"Oh, that," I say. "It's nothing."

"It's huge. How did you get it?"

"Who knows?"

Katie goes really quiet. "It was Jason, wasn't it?"

"No! Look, just because you don't like him doesn't mean he's a wife beater or anything."

"How did it happen, then? It's all big and purple and brown. Don't tell me you can't remember."

"Okay, if it makes you happier, I fell backwards and hit my back on a doorknob."

"Nobody falls backwards unless they're pushed."

"Quit with the social worker crap."

"I'll quit when you tell me who pushed you."

"It wasn't a push. Anyway, it was my fault. I was being mouthy and Jason just accidentally sort of bumped into me."

"Oh my god! What if you'd hit your spine? What if you'd broken your back?"

"Well, I didn't. Don't be so dramatic. It's only been once, anyway, and if you tell anyone—"

"What about those marks on your arms?"

"No big deal."

"Is this why you haven't been coming to gym?"

She's got me. I don't like getting hit, even if it's only been a couple of times and even if it's to teach me a lesson, like Jason says. But even worse than getting hit is the idea that other people might find out about it. They wouldn't understand. So I've been hiding my bruises with long-sleeved sweaters and jeans, which I've started to wear anyhow, on account of Jason doesn't like other guys staring at me. And I've also stopped going to gym. (Apparently Ms. Patrick thinks cramps can go on forever. Personal experience, no doubt.)

"I just bruise easy," I shrug.

"You do not. Leslie, you've got to stop going out with him."

I grab her by the elbows. "Mind your own business. Stuff between me and Jason is private. Okay?"

"You're getting beat up."

"Shut up!" I give her my hardest, hardest look. "Besides, aren't you supposed to be the big Christian? Whatever happened to forgive and forget?"

"This is different."

"It is not. Now swear you'll never blab." Her eyes are big and pleading, but no way I'm taking no for an answer. "Katie, if you don't swear, I'll never speak to you again. I mean it."

She bites her lip. "Okay," she says softly. She's almost crying. "But is it all right if I pray for you?"

"Fine. If it makes you feel better. Just don't tell me about it or I'll barf."

For the next few days, Katie keeps coming up to me all soulful and whispering, "Are you okay?"

Of course I'm not okay. I've never been okay. What's okay, anyway?

Life sucks. I want it to end.

Eighteen

It's one in the morning. I'm in my room writing this down, cuz if I don't I'll never sleep.

I am in unbelievably deep shit. It's about my journal. I should maybe just kill myself.

Breathe. Breathe.

Okay. To start at the beginning. Ms. Tracey James.

Ms. James arrived a week ago, last week of October. She's taking over from Ms. Graham, who won't be back until after Christmas. (Make that Christmas a couple of hundred years from now.)

Ms. James is under thirty. Real skinny, organized and scary. Like, when she introduced herself, Nicky Wicks made a fart sound with his armpit. Ms. Graham would've gotten flustered and the card players would've gone berserk. Ms. James just glanced at the seating plan and eyeballed him with a glare that'd stop a truck.

"Nicky," she said with this thin, crisp voice, "we're going to be seeing a lot of each other over the next few months. This experience can be pleasant or unpleasant. Your choice. What's it to be?"

Nicky shrunk into his desk.

"I beg your pardon?"

"Pleasant," he whispered.

Ms. James eyeballed him for another five seconds, then looked at the rest of us. "Are we all understood?" We stared at our desks, except for the card players, who quietly hid their decks.

"As for your mid-term reports," Ms. James said, "they're due at the end of next week. I'll be entering your grades for English once I receive a copy of your marks from Ms. Graham." Nobody's talking, but we're shifting in our seats. "What seems to be the problem?"

Cindy Williams flapped her arm like a wounded seagull. "Ms. James, we don't have any marks."

"What do you mean, you don't have any marks?"

"Ms. Graham never gave any tests or essays or anything, except for a content quiz and these question and answer sheets she never collected." Here Cindy showed off her binder, knowing the rest of ours were empty.

"If that's the case," Ms. James said, "tomorrow we'll have a test on *Mockingbird*, followed by an in-class essay, with automatic zeros for anyone missing without a doctor's note."

"But we haven't finished reading it," someone cried from the back.

"Then you'll have a busy night."

She got our tests and essays back to us within a day, which should put her in the *Guinness Book of World Records*. All the same, I only realized how big a marking maniac she is this afternoon. At the end of the period, she says she'd like to see me privately. Once we're alone, she tells me it's no secret she needs marks for our reports, so she's started to grade our journals.

"You're reading them?"

"Yes. And as you might guess, I find yours very disturbing."

"What?" I blurt out. "Ms. Graham promised they'd be private!"

"I'm sorry. I wasn't told."

"What kind of excuse is that?" I act all tough, but my stomach's heaving. Ms. James knows about me and Jason having sex, about me getting beat up, about, well, everything!

Ms. James pauses. "Leslie, do you understand the meaning of the word 'rape'?"

I can't breathe. "Yeah. So? What's it got to do with me?"

"It's what you wrote about."

"No, it's not." I struggle to my feet. "That journal is my property. Where is it? Give it back!"

"I can't."

"Yes, you can! Give it back or else!"

Ms. James stays calm. She's not mad, just very serious. "Leslie," she says, "I've given your journal to the principal. After this discussion, Ms. Barker wants to see us in her office."

"No!" I sink back into my seat.

Ms. James leans against the desk opposite. She looks concerned, but I hate her like I've never hated anyone. "I have an obligation to report abuse," she says. "You've been hurt. You need help."

"What's going to happen to Jason?"

"Leave that to the authorities."

That's when I throw up.

Because I'm sick, they let me go home. But the meeting with Principal Barker's still on for tomorrow.

Breathe, breathe.

I have to get my journal back. I have to make sure Barker keeps quiet about it.

If she doesn't, what'll it do to Mom?

And Jason. If I get him in trouble, what'll he do to me?

Nineteen

I'm in the office, on the bench opposite the secretaries' counter. It's where you wait till the principal's ready to see you. I stayed outside on the street till the bell, so I wouldn't have to talk to anyone in the halls. And I came to the office first thing so there wouldn't be any gossip about me getting called down. Please let no one guess anything's wrong.

I keep my head down, writing in my binder, pretending I'm invisible. God, please let Ms. James get here fast, so we can get this over with. And please—please—let Ms. Barker give me a break.

At our school, retired principals get places like the gym or the library named after them. In Ms. Barker's case it should be the office washroom. I picture this plaque over the flush toilet: "The Stella Barker Memorial Problem Solver."

Ms. Stella Barker. I call her Beachball.

I don't call her Beachball because she's all puffed up—which she is on account of I think she likes to drink. No, I call her Beachball because she rolls whichever way the wind is blowing. If it's convenient to say, "The grass is green," that's what she'll say. But if it's convenient to say, "The grass is blue," well, she'll say that too. She calls it being "flexible." I call it being a weasel.

For instance, last year there was this math test that by some miracle Cindy Williams forgot to study for. The minute she saw Mr. Kogawa handing out the questions, she had a panic attack and took off. Mr. Kogawa gave her a zero. But Cindy got all teary, said she'd been sick. He didn't buy it. So she went whining to her mother, who complained to Beachball that this zero would wreck Cindy's straight As.

Did Beachball side with Mr. Kogawa? No way. Cindy's mom is on the Parents' Council, so Beachball made the zero disappear, and Kogawa ended up looking like a fool. Cindy bragged all over that her mother told Beachball, "Either you deal with Fred Kogawa, or I go to the school board." Personally, if I was Cindy, I wouldn't brag about being a suck but, hey, whatever makes you feel important.

Anyway, two weeks later, I missed a geography test because Mom's alarm clock didn't go off. I got a zero too. So, I figured, no sweat, I'll do like Cindy's mom and talk to Beachball. Surprise, surprise: when I saw her in the hall, she wouldn't discuss it.

Beachball likes to tell parents that she "addresses individual student needs." Hah! She just plays favorites. That's why she can't stand Mr. Manley. He hands out suspensions no matter who your parents are. He's sort of an equal opportunity hard-ass. Beachball could care less if kids like me fail or get suspended. But kids whose parents can make trouble, that's another story.

Since Manley doesn't care about pushy parents, he makes headaches for Beachball. As a result, she bad-mouths him out loud to teachers in the corridor and tells her little pets they don't have to show up for his detentions.

Last year when Manley called Mom about my "absences," I asked how come she listens to him when the principal doesn't. Mom was shocked when I told her some of the things I've heard Beachball say. But she wasn't shocked at Beachball. No, she was shocked at *me* for telling "lies." According to her, Ms. Barker would never be so unprofessional. But she is. Ask anybody. She's a bitch with dimples. Ashley A-hole grown up.

Manley's a jerk, but he's a jerk to everyone. You know where you stand. The line is clear. But with Beachball, forget it. Logic and fairness are out the window.

That's why I'm scared about this meeting. There's no way to figure out what she'll do. Beachball might feel sorry for me and pretend nothing's happened. Or, she might call Mom and try to get me locked up.

Yeah, locked up. Last year, when I entered this "phase" I'm supposedly going through, Beachball invited Mom and me to her office. (Manley'd suspended me after I got nailed for forging Mom's signature on a school letter.) Beachball gave Mom a coffee and put on this caring routine, but what she really wanted was to get me tranked.

"We've found that students with hyperactivity, like Leslie, have benefited from Ritalin," she announced, as if she's a psychiatrist or something.

Lucky for me, Mom grew up in a small town. Even talk about drugs scares her. "I'd be a little uncomfortable putting Leslie on medication," she frowned.

("Hey, I'm sitting right here," I wanted to scream. I just love it when you're the topic of conversation and adults act like you're not even there.)

"These days medication is quite commonplace," Beachball soothed her. "To tell you the truth," and here she gave a little laugh, "half my staff are on anti-depressants." She meant that as a joke, but it wouldn't surprise me, the way she runs things.

"Well, it's something to think about," Mom said.

So on top of everything else, I'm worried maybe this time Beachball will go for broke and try to get me committed.

Ms. James waltzes into the office. "Leslie? I hope you're feeling better."

I shoot her a look.

The head secretary rings Beachball's private line. A few seconds later: "Go right in. Ms. Barker's ready to see you."

Twenty

*B*eachball doesn't get up when we enter her office. She motions for us to sit down, pulls my journal from the piles of paper on her desk and flicks it in front of me.

Silence.

She purses her lips like they're a pair of sugar tongs. "I must say you have quite a lively prose style." She makes a kind of grimace. I guess this is one of those jokes you're not supposed to laugh at. "You have scribbled any number of accusations," she continues, "allegations that could destroy a young man's life."

"No one was supposed to read my journal," I say, staring at the edge of her desk. "It was supposed to be private."

"Is that so?" Out of the corner of my eye, I see Beachball shoot a look at Ms. James.

"Please don't tell my mom."

"Your journal leaves us no choice but to tell your mother. And the child welfare authorities. And the police."

"The *police?*"

"They'll need to make a full criminal investigation. You should know that the McCreadys are unlikely to take these charges lightly. They may well lay charges of their own."

I flash on Mom collapsing, Jason in jail, me charged with something. "My journal's a lie! I made it all up!"

"Ah. So it's a fabrication?"

"Yes."

"It most certainly is not!" Ms. James interrupts.

"Says who?" I yell at her. "Who made you God?"

"Leslie, if you don't tell the truth, we can't help you."

"According to Leslie, she doesn't need help," Beachball purrs. "What she needs is to have her privacy respected."

Ms. James looks as if she's been sideswiped by a truck.

Beachball turns to me with a tight smile. "Might I suggest that in future you take more care with what you write. Might I further suggest that if you wish to avoid this fantasy becoming reality, you comport yourself with more discretion."

Ms. James goes ballistic. "Ms. Barker, surely you aren't suggesting that it's *ever* acceptable to be sexually assaulted."

Beachball's eyes narrow. "I'm afraid you haven't heard what I said."

"Maybe not, but I heard what you meant."

"I'm sorry you choose to misinterpret. In any case, this matter is no longer your concern."

It's like a Ping-Pong game, with me as the ball. I just want out. "So can I please have my journal back?"

Beachball puffs herself up. "You may. And I trust you will know what to do with it. Libel, defamation and slander are serious offences."

"You can't mean this is the end of it," Ms. James gasps.

Beachball pauses. "Close the door on your way out, would you, Leslie? I'd like to have a word with Ms. James." The last thing I hear before the door shuts is Beachball hissing, "You know, Tracey, in my experience, insubordination is not the best route to a long and happy career."

I put my journal in my bag and head to my locker. No way I'm going back to class. I slump on the floor.

Next thing I know, I'm staring at somebody's feet. I look up. It's Ms. James.

"Leslie," she says, "I want you to know, if you ever need help, I'm here."

I'm so mad at her for putting me through this. All the same, part of me wants to thank her. But if I did, I'd cry. So instead I just say, "Whatever."

Twenty-One

After Ms. James leaves, I stay by my locker worrying. How much should I tell Jason about what's going on? Maybe I should pretend this morning never happened. But there's always spies around, and I could have been seen in the office by kids going to the washroom, wandering the halls, you name it. Gossip could already be flying. If Jason hears anything, I could say I was taking the homeroom attendance down to the office or signing in late. But if someone saw me going through Beachball's door, he'll be on my case big time.

I don't get why Jason always has to know where I am and what I'm doing. He says I don't have to get it, it's just a fact. Since I'm his girl, he has a right to know everything. It's no use arguing, unless I want to get him mad. A few times, I've texted I'm somewhere I'm not. But it's like he's inside my head. "DONT LIE 2 ME!" he texts back, and I spill. Besides, when he explains why he needs to know, he sounds so sweet. "I love you. I worry about losing you."

"But if you love me, why can't you trust me?"

"I do. I don't trust other guys, that's all. They want to get into your pants."

"That's their problem," I tell him. "I'm not interested in anyone else."

"So if you're not interested, you've got nothing to hide. What's the matter, don't *you* trust *me?*"

When he puts it like that, I get mixed up. Then he holds me and snuggles me into his chest and kisses my hair and tells me, "I need to protect you. If I don't know what you're doing and you get into trouble, how can I look after you? I'd never forgive myself if you got hurt and I wasn't there."

"I guess."

"And, hey, speaking of trust," he says, "how do you think I feel when you lie about where you are?"

"Right. Sorry." It's not exactly what I'm thinking, but I'm too confused to say anything else, and besides, I don't want another bruise. Jason has no idea how strong he is when he grabs me, which is what he does when he wants to make a point. He's always making points.

So figuring what to tell him about my meeting with Beachball is really tricky. If I try to hide it, for sure I'll act paranoid and he'll know something's wrong. But if I tell him the truth, he'll go insane.

In the end, I don't have to decide. Right before the

period ends, he whips around the corner. "Get up. We're going outside."

"Sure. Just let me straighten up my locker."

He slams my locker door shut so hard it bounces back open and a couple of books fall out. "Is that straight enough?" He yanks me to my feet.

"Ow. What's with you?"

"Shut up."

I barely have time to grab my bag before he's hauling me down the hall by my elbow. A teacher sticks his head out of class to see what's going on. Jason drops my arm, but we keep moving.

"Sorry," I say to the teacher as we whisk by. "We're just going to the library."

Jason's walking so fast it's hard to keep up. But I know better than to fall behind. We're heading towards the south exit at the far end, away from the street, where the school hides its dumpsters. Nobody ever goes down there on account of it's all storage rooms, and once you step outside the door locks behind you. Basically the area's deserted except for late-night parties. In the mornings, the janitors have to check the alcove for needles, condoms and smashed beer bottles.

He kicks the door open and pushes me outside. "Okay, bitch, you got something to tell me?"

I try to stall. "What are you talking about?"

"Don't play games," he snarls. He bounces me off the wall. "What did you tell her?"

"Who?"

He makes a fist. "Barker. Don't play games."

"She called me in for skipping." I stumble backward towards the dumpsters.

"This is your last chance, bitch. What'd you tell her?" He grabs an old chunk of paving stone.

"No. Stop!" I trip. I scrape my hand on the gravel. I try crawling away on my right arm, shielding my head with my left. "Ms. James read my journal."

"What journal?"

"The one I've been doing in English."

"You wrote about me?"

"It wasn't supposed to get read."

"Answer the question." He squeezes the stone.

"Yes."

"Bitch!" He whips it over my head. It clangs off the dumpster.

"I'm sorry. I'm sorry!"

Jason rages towards me, his face all twisted. Oh god, help! I scrunch into a ball. He jumps on top, yanks my arms down, pins me.

"Get off me. Ow!"

"What did you write?"

"Just stuff."

"What stuff?" He knees my ribs.

"Leave me alone!"

"What stuff?"

"Nothing. Just stupid stuff."

He's right in my face now, talking hot and low. He's sweating like mad. "Well, that's real interesting. Because I had a talk with Barker too."

"What?"

"She called me in. Said there'd been a complaint. No names, but we all know who, don't we?"

"I didn't complain."

"Said I better be careful how I treat 'young women,' how I wouldn't want to get misinterpreted. What'd she mean by that?" He squeezes his knee in my gut.

"I don't know. Ow. You're crushing me. Someone's gonna see us."

"Big deal. You fell. I'm helping you up." He jerks me to my feet. "Last chance. What'd you write?"

Suddenly I don't care what happens. "I wrote what you do to me."

For a second, Jason goes calm. He chuckles, shakes his head and turns away. Then, before I know what hit me, he hauls off and smashes my shoulder. I crash back against the dumpster, crack my head, slide down into a heap.

"Where's your journal now?"

"In Barker's office," I lie.

"Get it back. I want it burned."

"I can't."

He boots the dumpster, to the right of my face.

Words spill out of my mouth. "I hate you! You're a pig! A pig! You're just like Katie said!"

"And you're a ho. A cum rag." He boots the dumpster again, closer.

"Go ahead. Kick me in the head. Kick me where people will see the bruise. Smash my face. Break my jaw. Why don't you, coward?" I can hardly believe what I'm saying. "You and me, we're finished."

"Oh, yeah? We're finished when I say we're finished."

"No. We're finished when I say. And I say now. It's over. O.V.E.R."

I expect him to go crazy, but instead he laughs. "Hey, the bitch can spell. I wonder if she can spell 'Sex Pix.'"

"What do you mean?"

"I mean the sex shots I took that first night when you were passed out. I think your mother'd like to see the kind of slut she raised. Flexible. I'm surprised you didn't make cheerleader."

"Hah!" My cheeks burn. "I checked your cell. There was just a stupid video of me dancing."

"On the phone, right. I saved the hot stuff to the memory card. I was upstairs hiding it when you came to. You think I want anyone finding out about my hobby?" He leans in, grinning. "Whenever I want, you're up on the Net, bitch. A spread-eagled porn star."

"You're lying."

"Try me."

He spits in my face and turns away. As he saunters off, he calls over his shoulder, "I'll be in the parking lot at three-thirty. Don't keep me waiting."

Twenty-Two

The books that fell out of my locker are probably being kicked up the hall by people changing class. But that's happening on another planet. I've only got one thing to think about besides throwing up, and that's getting to Jason's. Now, while he's out. If there's a memory card, I'm getting it back.

I leave the school grounds as fast as I can, grab a bus to the subway, take the subway to Sherwood station, then another bus to Jason's subdivision. Walking up his street, I feel like an alien. I imagine all these rich housewives and nannies watching me out of their living room windows, getting ready to call the cops.

Nobody walks around here. Even if they wanted to, there's no sidewalks, just curbs. It's like walking is a crime or something. Like, if you don't drive, you must be a lowlife casing a job.

Especially if you look like me. My jeans are ripped from the gravel, I'm covered in scrapes, my hair is a mess, and I've got a bump on the back of my head that feels like a watermelon. What'll I say when I see Jason's mother? "Hello, Mrs. McCready, your son's a rapist, but hey, who cares, have another drink"?

When I get to his house, her Camry's not in the driveway. Is she away, or just upstairs comatose, the car in the garage? I check my watch. It's not quite noon. I

can't believe she's out already; Jason told me she sometimes sleeps all day.

I ring the doorbell. It's one of those chimes that are
supposed to sound elegant but just sound phony, like the
ones at upscale shoe stores. No answer. I ring again. Still
nothing. Time for drastic action—I grab the brass door
knocker and bang away for all I'm worth.

Silence.

What now? I can't leave. Not without what I came for.
But with all the noise, the whole neighborhood must be
watching. If I try to break in, they'll call the cops for sure.

I get this wild idea. I wave at the empty living room
window, like there's somebody inside, then say in a loud
voice, "Oh hi, Mrs. McCready. You want me to meet
you in the garage? Okay."

What, am I crazy? Like that's supposed to fool anybody?

Relax. If the neighbors are nosy they'll have seen
me around here with Jason. They'll already be back to
watching TV.

I take a deep breath. The garage door lock's been broken
since Jason gave it a boot a month ago. I raise the door a
bit, slip inside and close it behind me.

I know the hiding place for the house key is under
the watering can by the garbage pail. Why do they even
have a watering can? As if Mrs. McCready'd be caught
dead holding one. As for Jason's dad, he's never home
long enough to water.

I let myself in. The warning from their security system starts beeping, but that's okay. Before the alarm goes off, I punch in the code and disarm it. I've seen Jason punch it so often, I know it by heart. 8-7-4-2, the last four digits of their phone number. What a stupid code. Like, do they *want* to get robbed?

Okay. I'm inside. The alarm is turned off. So far so good.

All the same, I'm afraid to move. Even though nobody's around to hear me, I'm terrified of making a sound. It's as if I think the furniture is alive, listening for intruders. How do guys steal for a living? Aren't they afraid to give themselves heart attacks?

I have a flash that maybe I'm not alone, that Mrs. McCready really is here, that she didn't hear me because she's downstairs working out on her X-Trainer. "Mrs. McCready?" I call out. "It's me. Leslie."

Silence. I'm alone.

I don't have much time. I better move fast.

Jason bragged he hid the memory card upstairs. That means his bedroom. Anyplace else, his folks could find it by accident.

I'm there in a heartbeat. But where do I look? How do I find it? It's barely the size of a dime.

I take a deep breath. Have to start somewhere.

I drop down, check under his bed, between his box spring and mattress. Throw over his rugs. Empty his desk. Shake out his books, knock over his lamps. Stand on a chair, run my hands above the wings of his ceiling fan. Tear the posters off his wall. No luck.

I turn to his closet. His mom does his clothes, so it's likely not there. But where else to look? I search the pockets of his pants, jackets. Rip out his drawers, toss socks and underwear everywhere. Reach to the back of his sweater shelves. Nothing.

On the closet floor, there's a cardboard box to the left, a tackle box to the right, and eight pairs of shoes in between. I shake out the shoes, throw them behind me. I rummage through the cardboard box, pitching the works: A baseball and glove. Ratty jockstraps. Condoms and lube wrapped in a T-shirt from Florida. But no memory card.

I'm down to the tackle box. I snap up the lid. I catch a quick flash of lures and fish hooks. And then—

The phone rings. My heart stops. It rings again. Silence. Either they've hung up or the voice mail's kicked in. I hold my breath as if somehow the person who's calling can hear me. Am I insane?

I glance around the room. Holy shit. It looks like a crime scene. It *is* a crime scene. No time to put things back. There'll be cops. I'll be charged with a B&E!

I panic. My legs fly me downstairs. I'm about to bolt out the door when I stop in my tracks.

The tackle box. The one thing I didn't empty. Jason doesn't fish. Maybe when he was a kid. But not now. It should've been stored away years ago. Unless he needs it for something. A hiding place. A place where a card the size of a dime could get lost in a pile of hooks and lures.

I run back upstairs. Grab the tackle box out of the closet. Spill the contents. Spread everything over the floor. I nick my thumb on a hook. Never mind. I see it. There. Beside a sinker. The memory card. With enamel paint for camouflage.

I race to the computer on Jason's desk. Stick the card in a card reader. An icon comes up on the screen, untitled. I click. Up come dozens of files with dates and first names. There's a file named "Leslie." Click. And there I am, sprawled with my legs open. There's close-ups, too, and other stuff that makes me sick.

I open the other files. They're of girls I've never seen before. They aren't in the downstairs rec room. They're posed someplace else. One of them isn't even in a house. She's outside, at what looks like the end of an old woods road with bushes and trees and shadows all around. It's night, and the light's coming from in front of her. I'll bet it's from the headlights of Jason's mom's car.

There's something familiar about these pictures. The way we look. Our age. Our hair. The way we're posed.

A sound fills the room, a kind of moan-roar coming from inside me. I start to rock. But I can't weird out. There's things to do. Like find out if Jason's copied our files to his hard drive.

I search "Leslie." Nothing comes up. Great. The porn's just on the memory card. I'm not surprised. I remember Jason's taunt: "You think I want anyone find-ing out about my hobby?"

I wonder how safe he plays it. I go to his Internet history, but he's cleared it. Is he hiding something? A blink and I'm at Bookmark Favorites. Not much to see: Yahoo, YouTube, Facebook, some standard game sites and something called "L.P. Peek-a-Boo."

Major sweat flash. "L.P." My initials! I click.

At first I don't understand what I'm seeing. The http address is my cell phone company. The left of the screen is full of ads. The middle is the Google Earth map. It shows Jason's street, centering over his home, with his house number underneath. Jason's name is at the top, next to my cell number. My cell phone's registered in his name, so fine. But why would he want to see a picture of his house? What's this site about?

I read the grid at the bottom of the screen: "Move-ments in Last Hour," "Last Day," "Last Week," "Last Month." I click "Last Hour." Up comes a pop-up map showing my route from school to here.

Oh god. I get it. The GPS chip in my phone has a tracking function. Jason's house is showing because that's where I am now. All those times he's asked where I am, it's all been a test. He's already known. He's stalked me on his computer.

Well, not anymore!

I slip the memory card in my pocket, and pitch the computer out his second-floor window. It smashes on the backyard patio stones, takes two bounces, and cannonballs into his swimming pool. Now that's what I call a computer crash.

As for my cell—I run to the hall bathroom and flush it down the toilet. Stalk that, you asshole!

Time to go. I'm losing it for real. I stagger down the hall to the top of the stairs.

I can hardly see. But I can hear all right. And what I hear is the front door opening.

Twenty-Three

I duck into the master bedroom, the nearest room available. Downstairs, the front door closes. Whoever's there puts something heavy on the floor.

"Jason?" It's Mrs. McCready. "Jason, are you home?" A pause. "That's strange."

What's she talking about? Of course. There's no alarm warning. I turned it off. Now what should I do: stay put or come out and hope for the best?

Just as I'm about to give myself up, I hear the sound of cans clattering and Mrs. McCready humming her way to the kitchen. Groceries. If she's gone to unpack them, she's not upset; she must figure she forgot to set the alarm when she left.

I hear cans hitting the counter. Good. If I slip downstairs real quiet, maybe I can make it out the front door before she's finished. After all, it's a new house with no creaks, carpet everywhere.

I step into the upstairs hall. I see the back of her legs heading into the living room. What a break! She didn't glance upstairs. I retreat back inside the master bedroom and stand stock-still, listening for clues about what to do next.

From downstairs, I hear someone talking. Mrs. Mc-Cready's listening to her voice mail on the speaker phone. And then ... humming. It's coming upstairs!

Should I run to the en suite bathroom? But what if she has to pee? I can hide behind the shower curtain. No, there isn't one; it's made of glass. At the last minute, I dive under the bed. I can see what's happening from a crack between the floor and where the eiderdown ends.

Flash. The door to Jason's room is open. What if she sees the mess?

But she isn't paying attention. She comes into the room. She walks towards me. She stops, turns and sits on the edge of the bed. She sits very still. I hear a gentle clink of ice cubes. She must be having a "tomato juice." I hear her set the glass down on the night table and sigh.

All this time, I'm staring at the back of her high heels. My brain's fried. Like, I'm having palpitations, but all I can think is: She wears high heels shopping? And now she slips them off. She stands up, walks to the closet and unzips her dress. She hangs it up and comes back to the bed in her bra and panties. She crawls under the eiderdown.

Oh no. She's taking a nap.

What do I do? I can't very well crawl out. But the longer I lie here, the more I worry about Jason. What'll happen if he comes home and I'm still here?

Lucky for me, Mrs. McCready can't sleep. Within minutes she's rolling over like a dog doing tricks. She lets rip a big ripe fart. I'm so amazed I don't know whether to gag or laugh.

"Lord," she mutters and gets up. I watch her put on her bathrobe, walk out of the room and head towards the stairs.

I wait just long enough to make sure she's really gone, then crawl out of hiding. Peek into the hall. The coast is clear. I tiptoe to the top of the stairs. Listen hard. No sound.

Here goes nothing.

I race down the stairs as fast as I can—and right into Mrs. McCready at the bottom.

She screams. Her left hand's clutched to her throat. Her right hand's clutched around another glass of "tomato juice." "Leslie!"

"Mrs. McCready!"

"What are you doing here?"

"School's out early. Jason said to come by."

"He's here?"

"No. He dropped me off. But he should be back soon. He's doing an errand."

She looks fuzzy. "How long have you been here?"

"I'm not sure."

Then it's like she sees me for the first time. "My god, Leslie, you're a mess."

"Am I?"

"Are you all right?"

I fake a laugh. "Oh, you mean my clothes and stuff. Today, at school, it was Hobo Day."

"Hobo Day?"

Talk about dumb. But I can't back out now. "We were supposed to come dressed like tramps. Student Council thought it'd be great for school spirit. We had to bring cans of food, too, for these boxes in the lobby we're donating to the Food Bank. I brought a can of spaghetti."

Mrs. McCready considers this. "What a wonderful idea." Thank god she's drunk.

"Yeah. It was lots of fun. But I better get going. I just remembered Mom needs me at home to help her clean up. She's having friends over for bridge."

"Why don't you wait till Jason gets back? He can give you a ride."

"That's okay. I can take the bus. I don't want to be a drag."

"Don't be silly."

"No, really. It's no big deal."

"Well, suit yourself." Mrs. McCready passes a hand vaguely across her forehead and stares into the air at a point somewhere behind the middle of my forehead. She's elegant, even in a yellow chenille bathrobe, all limbs and high cheekbones. But she's Botoxed to the gills, and her eyebrows are plucked and painted, which makes her look permanently surprised.

I must be hallucinating, because she doesn't even look like herself anymore. She looks like Ms. Graham. Ms. Graham with all the fat sucked out of her. Ms. Graham if she didn't have to worry about having a job. Ms. Graham all bewildered and too afraid to think or do anything.

Check please.

I wave like a maniac. "See you later," I babble, and scramble out the door while I still have a brain.

Twenty-Four

All the way to the bus stop, I'm scared I'll bump into Jason. It's barely two o'clock. He should still be at school, but what if he's skipping? What if he's gone online to check my cell's GPS site, to see where I am? What if he's here already, hiding someplace, watching me?

I keep an eye open for escape routes. If worst comes to worst, I figure I can cut across backyards. He wouldn't be able to follow on his motorcycle. But what if I'm cornered by somebody raking leaves? Or a pit bull?

I want to be home under the covers. But no way for that. The minute Jason sees his room, he's going to come after me. I picture me trapped in the apartment, with him in the hall trying to break down the door. Or the cops coming to arrest me after Mrs. McCready sees the chaos, not to mention the computer in the pool. No. Home isn't safe.

Besides, I can't go there with the memory card. I have to think of a hiding place. I want to destroy it, but I can't. If the cops come for me, it's all I have to stop the McCreadys from pressing charges. Not that I'd ever hand it over, but I could make the threat. Would that be blackmail?

All these thoughts zap my brain as I ride the bus to the subway. Once I'm at the station, inside, underground, I start to relax. If cops are after me, they won't look here. And Jason can't ride his bike down the escalator. Even if he did, what could he do to me in front of all these people?

As long as I stay where I am, I'll be fine. I buy an Oh Henry bar at the kiosk, sit on a bench and eat it, watching people get on and off the trains.

I wonder how long I could live here. I picture me holed up in a cardboard box somewhere down the tunnel, coming out early in the morning to stock up on Coke, chips, hot dogs and nachos. Once I'm reported missing, I'd have to watch out for people who might've seen my picture on a local news show. But it wouldn't be bad, apart from the rats and finding a bathroom: the subway toilets have been locked up for years.

Mom would be worried. But I could use the pay phone to leave a message saying I'm okay and I love her.

Just as I polish off my bar and get ready to toss the wrapper, I see these two subway patrol cops walking towards me. They look pretty grisly, like they don't get out much. What do they want?

I stare at the wad of gum squashed on the floor in front of me. If I stare hard enough, maybe I'll disappear. It works. The cops walk right past me and start hassling this guy playing guitar at the end of the platform. They're just like Mr. Manley, without teachers college.

When the train pulls in, I hop on. It's pretty full, but I find an empty seat at the end of the car. My back's protected. But not my mind. It starts playing tricks. I imagine the memory card falling out of my pocket, getting found, and then the pictures put on the Net.

Does being paranoid make me look suspicious? I concentrate on acting normal. But the more I concentrate on that, the more I freak.

Still, you can't freak forever. Without knowing when it happens, I zone out, bored, staring out the window at the tunnel and the stations flying by, until I'm sort of hypnotized. I'm like a zombie for I don't know how long, till my mind reboots.

I think about how if I didn't look at my watch I wouldn't know the time. So much has happened since this morning in Beachball's office, it could be years ago.

Time is just plain weird. When I was seven in Seattle, my Granny P. and Laura Wilson were at the center of my life. Now that Granny's dead, I only remember her in flashes, like snapshots, and Laura could be anywhere. It's like time keeps ticking, adding new people and things until sooner or later everybody forgets all about the old ones, even the old ones they used to care about.

I wish time was something I could grab hold of. I wish I could stop it from moving and making good things disappear. Still, on the plus side, it makes bad things go away too. Maybe someday it'll help me get over this nightmare called Jason.

Before every test, Katie likes to say, "This, too, shall pass." Actually, what she says is, "This, too, shall pass, even if we don't." Mom says something a lot the same: "Time heals all wounds." What with all the Dad stuff, I wonder if she still believes it. I don't. Time makes things go away, but it doesn't heal: it's more like an anesthetic.

I check the other passengers. Nobody's looking my way. They're all staring straight ahead, brain dead. It's like they walked in, sat down and went from Technicolor to gray. I'm in a train full of robots.

This idea makes me smile for the next three stops. Then I start obsessing about Jason again. It's like that for the next couple of hours. I go from scared to bored to giddy and back again as I sit riding the subway back and forth across the city.

Finally, I start getting lonely too.

I check my watch. It's almost five. Jason will've left school ages ago. Has he seen his room? What's he doing? (Swimming down the toilet after my cell, ha ha?)

I get off at the stop near Katie's and call her from the pay phone by the drug store.

"Hi, it's Leslie." I hear pots and pans and a bunch of people laughing.

"Leslie! Where were you this aft? I locked your locker. It was a mess."

"Katie, I have to talk to you."

"Sorry. My aunt and uncle are visiting from out of town. We're having a reunion. I'm supposed to entertain my little cousin."

"This is an emergency."

In the background, Mrs. Kincaid hollers, "Katie, get off your cell. Chloe wants to play with you."

"Okay," Katie calls out, then whispers, "I gotta go. I'll call you back later."

"You can't. I'm not at home. I don't have my cell. Katie, I'm not safe. I'm—look, if you don't see me again, it's because I'm dead."

"*What?*"

"I mean it."

"Where are you? Call the police. No, wait, *I'll* call the police."

"Call the cops and Jason'll kill me."

"Leslie, don't cry. Forget what I said. Come over right away. We'll—I don't know, we'll figure out something."

Twenty-Five

When I get there, Katie's out front on the sidewalk. She's got her cousin Chloe playing hopscotch. I'm pretty sure this is so I won't have to ring the doorbell and get intercepted by her mom.

Chloe looks like a glass of skim milk, all scrubbed and polished like she's going to church. Your basic trophy kid. The kind parents show off to make other parents jealous. I almost feel sorry for her. Instead of friends, I'll bet all she has is a bunch of stuffed animals. I picture her playing house with them, all alone in a cheery antiseptic bedroom plastered with Disney characters.

At the sight of me her lip wobbles and her eyebrows do the Wave.

"It's okay, Chloe," Katie says. "This is my friend Leslie. Why don't you go down to the basement and watch cartoons?"

Chloe does what she's told. Fast.

"Leslie! You look awful!"

"No shit." I tell her about the journal and Ms. James and Beachball and how me and Jason have broken up.

Katie's all excited. I know she wants to jump up and down, but these days she's making a big effort not to be so immature. She needs to work harder. This time, she shouts "Great!" at the top of her lungs.

"Don't." I shoot her a look. "I mean it. If you tell me God's answered your prayers, I swear I'll punch you."

"I'm sorry. Only I've been so worried."

"I know. Thanks." I tell her about the nude photos. I don't want to, but I can't help myself, I can't hold it in. Besides, she never blabbed about me getting hit.

Most of the girls at school would act shocked and give me a lecture. Then they'd ask to see for themselves. They'd pretend it was out of being a friend and wanting to share the horror, but really it'd be so they could act even more shocked and then run around telling everybody.

Not Katie. She gets very quiet, then hugs me.

Monster Mom sticks her head out the door. "Oh, hello, Leslie," she says, not even pretending to smile. "May I have a word with you, Katie?" Before Katie has time to get to the porch, her mom starts in. "Poor Chloe's sitting downstairs all by herself in front of the TV. Tell Leslie you'll see her some other time."

"But Mom—" Katie whispers urgently in her ear.

"That's nothing to joke about."

"I'm not."

"Fine. Ten minutes." She glares in my direction and disappears.

I want to die. "You told her?"

"Of course not. I said you were thinking of making a decision for the Lord."

"You told her *what?*" I see myself in a white robe

getting dunked in ice-cold water in the baptismal tub at Katie's church.

"Never mind. Let's get out of here. I'll tell her I was so busy hearing your witness I forgot about the time."

"She won't believe you."

"So? What's she going to do? Have a fit in front of my relatives?"

Now it's me with the bug-eyes. "You're lying to your mom? I must be a good influence."

Katie laughs as we hurry down the street. "I'm not as big a nerd as you think. I've started doing lots of bad stuff. In choir, half the time I don't even know the words. I just move my mouth and smile." Katie still has a ways to go in the sinning department, but I'm glad to see she's taking a few steps in the right direction.

As we walk, we talk about my problem: do I get rid of the memory card, or keep it in case I need to make the McCreadys back off about my B&E?

"First of all," she says, "you don't even know for sure if you're in trouble. Why don't you call home and find out?" Katie's pretty smart when she wants to be.

I use Katie's cell. Mom answers. I tell her I called in case she was wondering where I was. Mom's surprised. She thanks me for being considerate and says to hurry home because supper is about ready. I can tell she thinks I'm up to something.

Before she has a chance to ask me anything, I say, "Any messages?"

"Yes. Jason called. Something about missing you in the parking lot. But he said not to worry, he'll see you tomorrow about what you were looking for. What were you looking for?"

"Nothing. I'll be home right away. Bye." Click.

I'm having a hemorrhage, but Katie gets me to calm down. Obviously Jason knows I trashed his room and computer and stole the memory card. Equally obviously, he hasn't done anything about it. "And he's not going to," she says.

"Oh no? What about this 'see me tomorrow' bit? What's that supposed to mean?"

"He's trying to scare you. Come on, what can he say? 'Leslie stole the porn I made of a bunch of under-age girls?' I'll bet he's peeing himself wondering what you're going to do. Did you ever stop to think that maybe he called to find out if you'd told?"

I'm amazed. Who would have thought Katie could be so crafty? Anyway, according to her, I don't even need the memory card, as long as Jason thinks I have it. "Your only problem is if it gets found. If I were you, I'd ditch it. That way Jason's history, and you're home free. Before you know it, life will go back to normal, and you can pretend none of this ever happened."

That makes sense, except for the last part. I'm good at pretending, but not that good.

Together we take a vow of silence. I even let Katie say a prayer. Then I pull out my Bic and burn the card. We watch as the edges melt. I toss the charred remains down a drain hole.

All of a sudden, the pressure's gone. It's up in smoke. I can breathe again. I'm free.

I wish I knew who the other girls were. I wish I could tell them they're free too.

Twenty-Six

Next morning, I wake up thinking about Jason's message. I know Katie says to relax, but I can't. No way I want to see Jason till he's had time to cool down.

I cough loud enough for Mom to hear. "I don't feel well."

Mom comes into my room and touches my forehead. "You're fine."

"I'm not." Cough, cough.

Mom sighs, brings me the thermometer and goes to make breakfast. I rub it till it reads a couple of degrees high. Then I join her. "See?"

She knows I'm faking. She shakes it down and makes me do it again, this time watching me like a hawk.

"Do you mind?" I garble, lolling the thermometer around in my mouth. "I can do this myself, you know."

"I'm not stupid, and you're not skipping."

"I'm not skipping, I'm sick."

We fight all through breakfast. I make sure to cough

so much my throat hurts for real. As for Mom, she gets a headache. "Leslie, I don't have time to argue anymore. Get dressed. You're going to be late."

"You want me to infect the whole school? Talk about considerate. I hope it's meningitis. I hope I die, so you can feel guilty. I hope you get it too. That'll be a laugh, watching you hack away with double pneumonia."

She puts on her coat. "I'm not writing a note."

"Great. Get me expelled, why don't you?"

She leaves.

If you're going to skip, it's better to do it with a friend. Being stuck alone gets tired real quick. I flick around the TV. Nothing but news, cartoons and the Shopping Network. I wish I was stoned.

Then the phone rings. Is it him? If Mom weren't so cheap, we'd have call display. In case it's the school, I answer with my sick voice. Good move. It's the attendance secretary checking because I've been marked absent first period.

"I'm sick. My mom'll write a note."

"And what about yesterday? You left without signing out."

"I was too busy puking, do you mind? What are you? The CIA?" I hang up.

I turn off the TV. I walk around the apartment a couple dozen times. I make faces in the mirror. I'm so bored I even read the newspaper. The headlines, anyway. When I get this bored at Dad's, I sometimes watch the porno flick he keeps at the back of his filing cabinet under his old tax returns. I think it was a present from his stag party back when he married Mom. The hairstyles kill me, and the guys all have zits on their bums. I used to find it funny, but since all this stuff started happening with Jason, the thought of it makes me feel like heaving.

The phone rings again. I figure it's the secretary calling back. Or Mr. Manley. I answer with my sick voice. "I told you, I'm sick."

But it's not the school.

"You can't fool me, angel." Jason's voice is very even. "You took something of mine. I want it back. Plus your journal."

"I don't think so."

Pause. "Is your mother home?"

"What's it to you?"

A long pause. "I know where you live." Click.

I let myself down onto the couch and try to breathe. Is he coming over?

How can I keep him out? Our building doesn't have a doorman. The outside door downstairs is locked, but he could get in whenever a tenant comes or goes. I know. I've let in lots of strangers and seen others do it too. If they look respectable, you don't mind. If they don't, you don't want to get them mad.

The phone rings. I think it's him. It rings again. What if it's the school? Rings again. I'll say I was sleeping and didn't hear it. Rings again. And again and again and again, until I can't stand it anymore. I pick it up.

Silence on the other end of the line.

"Who is it?"

Breathing.

"I said, Who is it?"

Breathing.

I slam the receiver down and dial *69 to find the last number that phoned. I don't recognize it. I call anyway. It rings and rings and rings. Then someone picks up.

"Is that you, Jason?" I say, trying to keep my voice from shaking.

Silence.

"Listen, asshole, I'm calling the operator. You're in big trouble."

I hang up. I report the number. But there's nothing the operator can do. The call came from a laundromat.

This place is too creepy. I have to get out, go for a donut or something. I have a shower. Get dressed.

Just as I'm doing up my coat, there's a knock on the door. Help. I don't make a sound. Another knock. It's probably not him—but what if? "Who is it?" Silence. I tiptoe to the door. I check through the peephole. I can't see anyone. I keep the chain on and open it a crack. The elevator door down the hall is closing. The corridor's empty.

That's strange.

I take the chain off and open the door wide, ready to head out. And there at my feet is an envelope. My palms start to sweat. I open it. It's a Get Well card. There's a personal note inside.

"In sickness and in health,

Yours forever,

Love,

J."

I lock the door and stay inside for the rest of the day.

Twenty-Seven

That night, Mom and I keep our distance. She doesn't ask if I went to school, and I don't tell her I didn't. I'm going to school tomorrow, though. I have to face him sooner or later, so I might as well do it with other people around for protection. And besides, hiding out breaks my Number One Rule for trouble at school or at home: Never let them see you're scared.

I get to school minutes before the bell rings. Katie, Ashley and the others are talking at the lockers. Katie gives me a smile and a finger-wave. She's about to say something when suddenly her eyes go wide, like they do when she's watching horror movies. I turn. It's Jason.

"What do you want?"

"Don't I even get a hello?"

"As in, go to Hell-o?" I say it loud, so everyone will be watching in case he tries to yank me away.

But he doesn't. He shakes his head, sad and soulful.

"There you go again. That's exactly why I broke up with you."

For the first time in my life, I'm speechless.

"You gotta do something about your attitude," he goes on. "Not to mention the other stuff."

"What are you talking about?"

"Do I have to say it in public?" He pretends to whisper, but it's loud enough for everyone to hear. "Last Saturday? That guy feeling you up at the club?"

"You are such a liar."

"Whatever you say. I don't care anymore. I've had it." Jason glances around at the eavesdroppers. They look away, embarrassed. Except for Ashley. He flashes the baby blues and winks at her. "Hi." Then the jerk swivels and saunters off down the hall.

Ashley acts casual, but I know how she's feeling.

"Don't," I warn her.

"Don't what?" she smiles, all innocence.

"Just don't."

"You're not my mother."

"He's not what you think."

"How do you know what I think?"

"Trust me."

"As if." And she struts off to class with her nose so high I picture it scraping the ceiling.

Katie takes my arm. "Even if we told, she'd never believe us," she says in my ear. "Besides, it's not like he asked her out or anything."

Let's hope it stays that way. I don't want anything on my conscience.

By the end of school, I've relaxed. I even figure Jason flirting with Ashley is good news, because it means he's not taking the breakup so hard after all. Who cares if he pretends it was me who got dumped? He's off my case. That's what I'm thinking on my way home, anyway. The idea makes me so happy I turn my music way up and sing along.

I'm so into this other world I almost bump into him. He's jumped the curb on his motorcycle and blocked the sidewalk. I pull out my earphones. "What do you want?"

"We have things to talk about."

A heartbeat, then loud and firm: "You're not getting it back. And if you don't leave me alone—right now—I'm taking it to the cops."

"Sure you are," he mocks. "You don't want people seeing those pictures any more than I do."

I toss my head. "Don't count on it."

He smiles. "I admire your guts, breaking into my room like that, busting my computer. Mom saw me haul it out of the pool. Told her I tripped carrying it across my room, and it fell out the window. She bought it."

"She'll buy anything."

"Great, eh?" He grins. "Explaining your cell was tricky, though. It plugged our toilet. Nice touch. I have a whole new respect for you."

"Save it for someone who gives a shit." I start to move around him.

"Hey, come on, don't be such a tease."

I'm past him.

"Where're you going?"

I don't answer. I don't look back. I move fast. He revs his engine. He starts following me, slow, motor almost idling. He could run me down if he wanted. "You're not supposed to be on the sidewalk," I say, hard.

He laughs, guns his motorcycle onto the road, races to the end of the block and wheels around to face me. I turn and start walking back the way I came. I hear him gun the engine. He rides past me, turns back up onto the sidewalk and faces me again. "Fancy meeting you here."

"Get lost, Jason."

"That's my girl," he winks. "Make me hot."

I spit at him, but nothing comes out. My mouth's too dry.

"I wouldn't do that again."

"Oh, really? You want to beat me up on a public street? Go ahead. There'll be witnesses. I wouldn't be surprised if someone's watching out their window right now."

"There won't always be witnesses."

"What's that supposed to mean?"

His eyes go dead. "I love you, Leslie," he says. And with that, he revs his engine. Before I can think to scream, the motorcycle lurches towards me. At the last second, it swerves back to the road and he takes off.

I phone Katie the minute I get home. I can hear her swallow. "He's probably playing games. Pretty soon he'll get bored and move on."

"Or do something."

"Don't talk like that. It scares me."

"You've never seen that look of his. So far, okay, maybe it's all been a game. But what happens when he figures he's lost? Jason doesn't lose. Ever."

"You're psyching yourself out. He may be a bully, but it's not like he's killed people or anything."

"Yet."

Actually, "yet" is what I want to say, but I don't have the nerve. Instead I mumble, "Yeah, you're right."

There's a silence. Then Katie says, "You're not alone, you know."

"I know."

"Love you."

"Me too."

Twenty-Eight

Nothing much else has happened for the past week. It hasn't had to. The idea that it might is just as bad. And I can't stop thinking about the possibilities because wherever I turn, it seems like Jason's there.

He's smart about it. He doesn't get too close. But

he's always around just the same. In the corridors. Outside my classrooms. At the door to the gym. A couple of tables away in the library. By the pop machines in the cafeteria. Always with that smirky smile and that cool slouch. Sometimes his shades are on, so I can't tell for sure if he's looking at me. But he is.

Luckily, I have Katie. She's dropped everything, including Ashley, to be with me after school. (She's told her mom she's making props for the drama club.) We put in time until I know Mom'll be back from work, and then Katie walks me home.

For waiting, we mostly go to this little park near the school. It's getting cold, but we huddle up on a bench and watch the world go by. People walking dogs. Kids rollerblading. Moms, some my age, pushing baby carriages. And every so often, a bunch of geriatrics with walkers. They come on outings from the local old folks' home. By the time they all get off the bus, it's time to get back on.

These days I'm a real downer. I don't know how Katie puts up with me, I'm so insane. Like, I hate Jason, but sometimes I find myself missing him, too. Every so often I tuck my head in, squeeze myself into a ball and sob. Katie puts her arm around me and pats my shoulder until I stop. Maybe Beachball was right. Maybe I should go on tranks or something.

Katie tries to cheer me up. "Being happy isn't easy. You have to work at it." Talk about cornball. But Katie looks so serious I can't help smiling. "See. A smile. Good. Now how about a laugh? 'Laugh and the world laughs with you.' That's what Mom says."

"Your mom is mental."

"Come on, Leslie. Remember when you first came here, how you hated leaving Seattle and how miserable you were?"

"Earth to Katie: I'm still miserable."

"Yeah, but you're not crying about being homesick anymore."

"Only because I have better things to cry about."

"You know what I mean."

"Yeah, I know what you mean. But, Katie, maybe I don't feel like being happy right now. Okay?"

"Okay."

And we sit there, shivering, until it's time to go home.

I haven't told Mom about the breakup, but she knows. I can tell because she's extra nice all of a sudden. Like, even though I haven't been eating much, she hasn't made a big deal about it or given me a lecture about anorexia. She hasn't asked me to clear the table either. Best of all, she hasn't asked questions.

Last night was a close call, though. She's scraping plates before doing the dishes when out of nowhere she stops, wipes her hands and comes over.

I'm still at the table staring into space, twisting a napkin. Mom puts her hands on my shoulders. I don't look up. "What?"

"You know, honey," she says in her Sympathetic-Mom voice, "somehow things have a habit of working out for the best." That's one of the biggest lies in the world, but part of me likes her saying it, because it means she cares. The other part of me gets mad, because even though the breakup makes me feel terrible, I know it makes her feel great.

I guess I should be grateful. She could have said, "I know how you're feeling" or "Don't say I didn't warn you."

I shrug off her hands and get up. "Want some help with the dishes? I can dry."

"That'd be nice," Mom says, totally stunned. "Thanks."

If she wasn't my mother, I might even like her.

This morning when I get to school, everything's normal except for one thing—Jason's nowhere in sight. By the end of the day, I'm starting to have a good time. Maybe I am being paranoid. Maybe I don't need a bodyguard after school.

I get back home feeling great, grab a snack and sit down to check my e-mails. There's one from Jason headed: "Hi there stranger." Inside there's attachments. I click.

Oh god. It's photos of me and Katie in the park.

Twenty-Nine

I forward the e-mail to Katie. She calls right away. "You still think I'm paranoid?" I say.

Katie tries to control her breathing. "Mom always says if you ignore teasing it'll go away."

"That's what every adult says, and it's a lie. Do nothing and things get worse."

"I know," she says in a scared voice. "But what choice do you have? You can't stop him going where he wants. You can't stop him taking pictures."

She's right. I decide to pretend everything's fine, hold my breath and hope for once her mother is right.

She isn't.

Jason works like magic. I never see him. But at least twice a day, when I open my locker, a card falls out with a cheesy message like "You Complete Me." On the Net, I've changed my Facebook settings and deleted him from my Friends list, but my regular in-box is swarmed with e-mails from strange addresses, headed, "Hi there Leslie" or "UR Hot 2Day Leslie," and photos of me at the corner store or coming home. I change from Gmail to Hotmail to Yahoo. It doesn't matter. Within a few days, he's found my new address and the swarming starts again. Honest to god, just going online gives me a rash, and I shake so bad at my locker, it takes forever to land my combination.

Then there's the phone. It never stops ringing. I let Mom answer. When it's him, there's just a click. Like me, she dials *69. The number's always blocked.

We turn off the ringer at night. I mean, he's even called at two and three in the morning. The first couple of times, Mom hurried to answer, thinking it was some emergency. I finally told her it's Jason.

"You don't know for sure." That's what she said, anyway. I guess she doesn't know what to do either.

After two weeks, it's all too much. I open my locker before school and out drops another card. I sink to the floor a nervous wreck. And there he is, lounging against the wall opposite, grinning at me.

"Go away!"

He gives this innocent shrug. "What did I do?"

I'm too freaked out to say anything. But not Katie. She walks right up to him and sticks out her chin. "You know, if you really cared about Leslie, you'd leave her alone!"

"*Me* leave *her* alone? She's the one who won't let go. Calling my place all the time, sobbing to my mother." A glance at me. "I wish you'd stop it, Leslie. It's getting tired." He sounds so sincere, I can't believe it.

"You put cards in my locker," I whimper. "You swarm me with e-mails."

"What are you talking about?" he laughs. "Are you sending yourself cards and e-mails now? No wonder people think you're a nutbar." He cocks his head at

Ashley. "Actually, she's the reason I dropped by." He smiles at her. "I'll catch you later, Ash, when Twitch-Brain's had her meds." He gives her his famous finger-point, grins and heads off.

Ashley pulls out her books really fast.

"Don't go after him," I say. "He's a rapist."

"She's right." Katie nods.

"And you're a liar and a baby suck," Ashley snaps and hurries off. *Baby-suck.* This from someone whose mom won't let her wear eye shadow.

Thirty

I don't eat lunch. I sit with Katie, then go to math. I'm actually looking forward to it, because math puts me to sleep, and sleep is what I need. I usually leave mid-class to snooze in the can, but today I just put my head on the desk.

As always, Mr. Kogawa does his impersonation of a human being, droning away, solving problems on the board and wiping the chalk off with the sleeve of his jacket. But even though I'm dying to pass out, I'm so wired it's like I'm on Red Bull. All I can think about is Jason. I need some privacy. I put up my hand, Mr. Kogawa waves me off, and in a couple of minutes I'm in the far cubicle of the girls' second-floor washroom. I figure I'll stay till school's over.

After I've read the graffiti for the millionth time, I start to nod off—till out of nowhere, I feel the hairs on the back of my neck stand up. It's the weirdest thing. Like when I pick up the phone to call Katie and she's already on the line. Or when I'm in a place for the first time but it's like I've been there before. Or when I can feel that I'm being stared at.

Like now.

I lean over and check the floor on all sides outside the cubicle. No feet. Of course not. The can was empty when I got here, and no one's come in since. I'm just freaking myself out. I sit back down, take a few deep breaths. Then this long, slow horror fills me. What if the stare is coming from above?

I look up, afraid of what I'll see. Sure enough, there he is. Jason. He's standing on the toilet lid in the cubicle next to me, staring down.

I want to run for it. But if I do, he could hop out and grab me. So I sit there, frozen, like a mouse in front of a snake.

"You're late," he whispers.

"What ...?" I struggle to breathe.

"You're usually here by one-thirty."

"You've been hiding there all along?"

He smirks. I feel sick.

"It's your own fault," he says. "How else am I supposed to talk to you? You hang up the phone. You don't even say thanks for the cards."

"I thought you wanted Ashley."

"Got you jealous, didn't I?"

I want to say, In your wet dreams, pencil dick, but I bite my tongue. "You better get out of here. Someone could catch you."

"So what? If they do, you'll be the one in trouble."

"Pardon?"

"I'll say you brought me in here for sex."

My lip quivers.

"Come on, Leslie, don't be like that. I only wanted to teach you a lesson. I miss you. I need you." And now he talks like a Hallmark card, like he used to do after he'd hit me. How his life was nothing before he met me and I'm his "special someone" and he's so sorry and blah blah blah. "I mean it, Leslie," he pleads, "without you I'll die."

"Good!"

"Good?"

"Yeah. Go ahead and die." Saying it feels great. So great I don't even think about the consequences. I keep going, getting braver with every word. "What use are you, anyway? You just waste space. So go ahead. Jump off a building. Swallow a medicine cabinet. You think I care?"

Jason's face contorts. For an instant, I think he's going to cry. Then—wham wham wham—he smashes the wall of the cubicle with his fist. I squinch my eyes and raise my hands as if his fist could break right through.

He crashes out of his cubicle. He stands in front of my door. He gives it a boot. It shakes on its moorings. He boots it again. And again.

Just when I think it's going to break off its hinges, he stops. "You'll be sorry," he whispers through the crack. Then he turns on his heel, like nothing's happened, and walks out whistling.

Thirty-One

The e-mails and phone calls have stopped. But not the cards. Just three this past week, but that's enough.

Katie says it's a sign he's getting bored; a few more weeks and he'll leave me alone for good. I wish I believed her, but I don't. These cards are different. Instead of being full of sucky love crap, they're the kind you get after a death in the family—"In Memoriam," "Deepest Sympathy," "With the Angels."

"Leslie, if you really think they're death threats—tell!"

"Tell what? There's no handwriting. Nothing to prove they're from him. If I say anything he'll deny it and I'll get accused of being sick, of trying to get attention, of acting out."

Then, last Monday, I opened my locker and there was a dead mouse on top of my books. I screamed.

Some other girls screamed too; a few guys laughed.

Later, Katie tried to reassure me. "I doubt if it's from Jason. You're lucky you haven't had mice before, with all those old sandwiches squashed under your gym bag. Besides, he doesn't have your combination, does he?"

"I don't think so."

But I change my lock all the same.

Meanwhile my marks have been going to hell. I can't concentrate to study, and as for doing homework, please. Apart from math, which I can do in my sleep, my only decent mark is English.

Katie's marks are down too. Her mom says it's my bad influence and it's got to stop, especially now that exams are coming. That means Katie and I can't spend time together after school; she has to study.

At least she still walks me home, right up to my apartment. And she waits till I've checked the closets and under the beds, too. She says if Jason comes by and starts pounding on the door before Mom gets back from work to call her right away. As if Katie could do anything over the phone.

The worst part of being home alone is having time to think. I think about horrible stuff. Like how last winter there was this teenager out west who got stabbed to death and dumped in the bushes. It took months before they found his body; and when they did, it turned out practically all the kids from the local high school knew he was there, they just hadn't told anyone. The adults on

TV acted shocked about how the kids could have kept this awful secret. Adults can be pretty stupid.

If I get murdered, I hope Mom won't be mad at me. It's not as if meeting Jason was my fault, exactly. I don't know what it was. Bad luck? Fate? Or maybe God answers prayers after all, to teach people a lesson. I don't know. It doesn't matter. Nothing does.

Katie says it's sick to talk about this, but if Jason kills me, I want to be cremated. I can't stand the idea of being stuck in a box forever. It makes me claustrophobic. I'd like my ashes to be kept in the stone jar we got from Granny P. on her last visit before she died. Mom could keep it on the kitchen counter by the window, next to the African violets. Or, if seeing me there all the time would make her sad, I guess she could store them in a closet. Whatever. I just don't want to get buried or scattered.

If you ever read this journal, Mom, I hope you can forget all the awful things I said to you. I didn't mean them. I'm sorry I was a disappointment.

Thirty-Two

In slasher flicks, when a babysitter's alone and hears a strange noise coming from the attic, she always checks it out—even when she knows there's a psycho prowling the neighborhood who goes after babysitters in attics. If Katie and I are watching the movie together, I always elbow her as the babysitter climbs the creaky stairs and her flashlight goes out. "Here comes the chainsaw."

"Tell me when I can look," she squeals, peeking through her fingers.

Part of me thinks those babysitters deserve to die for being so stupid. But the other part of me knows why they do it. It's because the door at the top of the stairs is alive with this overwhelming question: What's on the other side? That question pulls them to their deaths like they're zombies.

I'm in my room cramming for Friday's geography exam when the phone rings. Nothing bad's happened for two days, and I'm getting calm enough to memorize all about semi-arid continental climates.

Mom answers. "Hello? Oh hello, Jason. I'm sorry, but she doesn't want to speak to you."

I perk up. Jason? He identified himself?

"I'll give her the message." Mom sticks her head in. "That was Jason."

I twirl my hair with my pencil and keep staring at my textbook like I couldn't care less. "What did he want?"

"Not much. He called to say goodbye. He says he's been thinking it over, and he's taking your advice."

"Oh," I say absently, but chills run up my spine. My only advice to Jason was to kill himself. He's doing it? He's called to say goodbye?

"Is he changing schools?" Mom asks.

"I guess so," I yawn.

"Well, that's good. An odd time, though, right before exams."

"An odd time for an odd guy."

Mom laughs. "I'm glad you have your sense of humor back." She gives me the kind of Earth Mother Look that makes me want to hurl. "The first breakup's always tough. But I told you you'd get over it. You know, I remember when I was sixteen—"

"Yeah. Chester Martin. You loved how he hiccuped. You've told me. I'm studying."

"Sorry." And she disappears.

After a quick panic, I reassure myself. No way Jason's going to kill himself. He just wants to wreck my studying. I won't let him.

I try to go back to reading. But I can't. I keep thinking, what if I wake up tomorrow and he's dead? What if those funeral cards weren't about me? What if they were about him? What if they were a cry for help? He's a creep and I hate him, but if he dies, how will I live with myself?

I decide to phone. If he's really killing himself, maybe I can talk him down or get an ambulance. But I can't call from here. I don't want to risk Mom listening in on the extension, like I do when she's talking to Dad. There's a pay phone at the end of the street.

"I need a break," I say, grabbing my coat. "I'm going for a walk to the corner store, maybe pick up some gum."

"Oh, could you get milk while you're there?"

"Sure."

She gives me some money.

"Back in a few minutes."

All of a sudden I get this crazy thought. What if Jason can read my mind? Like, what if his call is part of a plan to get me outside now it's dark? What if he's waiting in the bushes? Hardly anyone's on the street at night, and I have to pass a couple of alleyways and—this is nuts, just me flipping out. Am I a prisoner in this dump or what?

All the same, to be safe, I go back to my room and write a quick note: "If anything happens to me, it's Jason." I put the note on my desk under my geography book. That way Mom won't walk in and find it by accident, but it's there just in case.

Outside, I walk fast, crossing the street whenever I get near an alley. They're all empty, except for one with a kid huffing airplane glue out of a paper bag. "You're gonna get zits all around your lips," I shout across the street. He looks up sort of glazed. "Yeah," I go on, "and then your brains are gonna fall out!" Okay, I've done my bit to save his life, now time to think about saving Jason's.

I get to the pay phone feeling like a total drama queen. I make the call. The phone rings forever. At first, my chills come back—is Jason somewhere around here watching? But the longer it rings, the more I start to wonder if maybe it's true about him killing himself—and if he's maybe already done it. Shot his brains out. Slit his throat. Hung himself. Should I call the cops? Call his cottage? Call a cab?

I'm about to hang up and call *somebody*, when he finally picks up. "Hello?" He doesn't sound so good, but maybe he's acting.

"What's your message supposed to mean?"

"Leslie, Leslie, it's you. I'm glad you called. I wanted to hear your voice one last time. My parents are at the cottage. Tonight's the night."

"For what?"

"I've got a quart of Jack Daniels and a bunch of my mom's pills. Thorazine, Lorazepam, ludes. You'll never have to see me again."

"Come on, Jason. No way you're killing yourself."

"Let's not fight."

"Look, I don't have time for this. I have an exam tomorrow."

"Then go home and study." His voice gets groggier. "I've left some stuff for you on the rec room pool table."

"What stuff?"

"A letter. About how you were right. How I don't deserve to live."

"You left a letter blaming me?"

"It doesn't blame you. It thanks you. You made everything clear."

"That's sick."

"There's also a copy of that memory card of you and the other girls. You never found it cuz it wasn't in the box with the original. I kept it in my wallet so I could see you naked whenever I wanted. I've put it in an envelope addressed to the cops, with all your names and addresses. Maybe you can pass it on."

"Oh god, no, Jason, no. Destroy it now."

"Goodbye, Leslie."

"I said, destroy it!"

But it's like he doesn't hear me. "Have a good life. I loved you. I'll watch over you forever." Click.

I hear the dial tone. For a second, I freak. Then I'm pissed. He's playing mind games. What kind of fool does he take me for?

I go into Happy Grocery breathing fire, pay for the milk and ask for a pack of smokes. The cashier asks for my ID.

"I don't have it with me."

"Then sorry."

"Don't *sorry* me!" I yell. "You're the only stupid store in the whole world that asks for ID, so get real."

The woman grabs a broom and tells me to get out or she'll call the cops.

"Happy Grocery, my ass," I snarl, and take off.

I go back to the pay phone, ready to rumble. I call Jason again. It rings I don't know how many times. I picture him laughing to himself as he listens. Then I picture him slipping into a coma from his mother's pills and booze. I go from mad to scared. I think about phoning the suicide prevention line or even the cops, but I can't take the chance. What happens if there really is a note and a memory card for the cops? There'll be an investigation. Mom'll find out. I'll be called a whore and a murderer.

I pace outside the phone booth, talking to myself. It seems to help me think. I remember to whisper and not move my lips. I don't want to attract attention, like Marge with the shopping cart outside Katie's church.

"What's the big deal? Just go over," I say.

"What, are you crazy?" I answer back.

"If Jason dies and you don't go, you'll blame yourself as long as you live. Plus, going means you'll get the only remaining copy of the porn plus the letter."

"But what if he's bluffing?"

"He won't do anything while he thinks you may have the memory card. He hasn't touched you since you stole it, has he? And you left that note in your room for insurance."

It's settled. I'm going over. But not alone.

I call Katie's cell.

"Hellew." It's Mrs. Kincaid, using her classy voice.

"Hi, it's Leslie. Can I please speak to Katie?"

"I'm afraid Katie is studying for her exams."

"I know. But this is an emergency."

"It will have to wait till tomorrow."

"But—"

"Goodbye, dear." Click.

So Katie's cell is confiscated. I wait a minute and call

back on the Kincaid's landline, hoping to get somebody besides the Witch.

"Hellew?"

I hang up. Another few minutes, and I call again.

But Mrs. Kincaid knows this game. "Leslie, am I going to have to speak to your mother?"

I hang up. I guess I'm going by myself after all.

There's a drunk passed out on a nearby park bench. I leave the milk from Happy Grocery next to his booze and grab a passing cab. I can pay with the change from the twenty Mom gave me. Lucky I didn't get smokes after all. Was that fate? Or a guardian angel?

Mom'll be wondering where I am. She'll be worried and mad. But I don't have time to think about that. I'm on a mission of life and death.

Thirty-Three

The cab pulls up in front of the McCreadys'. There aren't any cars in the driveway, the curtains are drawn, no lights. I ask the driver to wait, but he's a little suspicious and wants to see some money. I've only got enough for the ride, which leaves me with two quarters. He swears, tells me to get the hell out and takes off.

I go up the walk, ring the doorbell. Nobody comes. I rap the brass knocker. The front door opens by itself. It must have been ajar.

It's pitch-black inside. There's light switches on the wall to the right. I reach in and flick them all on. Then I step in, leaving the front door wide open.

"Jason?"

Silence.

I take a second to think. The note and the memory card are supposedly on the pool table in the rec room, but they can wait. The first thing I have to do is find Jason. If he's dying, I need to call emergency right away. If he's not, I don't want him coming downstairs after me, trapping me in the basement.

I figure if he's taken pills, he's probably upstairs on his bed. That's where I'd be if I was going to OD. First, to be comfortable. Second, to be considerate to Mom. "She looks so peaceful, just like she's sleeping," she'd think. Even if that's not a great comfort when you realize the person's dead, it beats finding them with their bum sticking out of a gas oven and the house ready to blow. Or with their brains decorating the wallpaper.

The idea that Jason may be in a coma makes me want to run up to his bedroom right away. But in case it's a trap, I say in a loud voice, "You stay behind that bush, Katie. If I'm not back in two minutes, call the cops." Then I check the main floor, peeking in obvious hiding spots like the front hall closet and turning on all the lights as I go, even the lamps and the little light over the stove. On top of that, I check the garage and poke my head out the back door. He's nowhere.

Now for his bedroom. "Just another two minutes, Katie," I call out. Then I go to the foot of the staircase, flick on the upstairs hall light and head up.

I hurry to his room at the end of the corridor. Along the way, I glance into the other rooms in case he's inside one of them, waiting to pounce. The rooms are dark. But empty. I turn on their lights and keep moving.

And now I'm at his door. It's shut tight. "Jason?" I throw it open. What a mess. But no Jason.

I get a panic flash that he's back down the hall hiding in his parents' en suite bathroom. I imagine him blocking my exit and—zoom—I fly down the stairs, three at a time, and race out the front door, gasping for breath.

Home free. I fall on the grass and laugh. I feel a bit hysterical from sheer relief.

But it's not over yet. There's still the basement—the furnace, laundry and rec rooms. And in the rec room, the pool table, where he said I'd find the memory card and the note.

No problem, I tell myself. There's lights everywhere now. The front door is open. I have a clear, well-lit escape route.

"Okay, Katie, keep me covered." It occurs to me I might be giving the neighbors a show. I look across the street, but the living rooms are all either dark or have their curtains drawn. Right. Around here everyone has families, and family rooms at the back of the house to put them in.

I take a deep breath and go back inside. I get to the basement stairs and start down. Something feels wrong. Like I'm going into a burial vault.

"Turn back," I tell myself.

But my feet won't listen. That memory card is so close. A few more steps and I'll have it. That porn of me will be gone forever. Even if this is a set-up, Jason won't do anything as long as he thinks Katie's outside.

So I keep going, like one of those zombie babysitters.

I'm at the rec room door. It's wide open. Inside, everything's dark. I feel for the light switch, half afraid Jason's going to grab my hand.

I find the switch. Click. Light floods the room. Good—he's not here. I start towards the pool table, but there's nothing. No note. No memory card. Oh god. It is a trap! I shouldn't have come. And now, from upstairs, the sound of the front door closing. Footsteps. The sound of the basement door closing. And somebody coming down.

It's Jason.

He enters the rec room slowly, shutting the door behind him. "Hi." No smile. Nothing.

Don't show him you're scared, I think. "So you're okay. I was worried."

"I'll bet."

"Really," I stammer. "So where's the copy of the memory card?"

"There isn't one."

"Oh," I gulp. "Well, if there's no backup, and you're okay, I better get going."

He doesn't move from the door. "You're not going anywhere."

We stand there for I don't know how long, squaring off. Then I hear myself say, "Katie's outside. Let me go or she'll call the cops."

"Right. I watched through the curtains. You came by yourself."

My stomach flips up my throat. "Where did you hide when I first came in? I looked everywhere."

"Behind the furnace. I figured you'd head to the rec room right away, but you're full of surprises." His lip twitches. "When you ran out, I went to see what was up. I was right behind the front door when you came back in."

"Well, ha, ha, ha, aren't you clever." I struggle to act sarcastic. "Is that supposed to make me scared?"

A flicker in his eyes. "You're pretty smart for a dead girl."

"Very funny."

But he isn't laughing.

"Okay, you win. Now let me go. I've got that memory card, remember? If I get hurt—"

"If you get hurt, so what? That memory card is history."

"Says who?"

"Me. You're too chicken to keep it. Not that I care.

I mean, who's to say I took those shots? And if I did, so what? Photography's my hobby. You wanted to pose. It's just private boyfriend/girlfriend stuff. Anyway, Dad'll fix any problems. He always does." Jason smiles. "Nobody makes a fool of me. Especially not some skank. Some pig ho slut. Who do you think you are, anyway?"

He starts to move around the pool table. I move too, keeping it between us. "Don't, Jason," I scramble. "Even if Katie's not outside, she knows I'm here."

"Big deal. You may be here, but I'm not. I'm up at the cottage with my folks. Ask them. Wanna bet what they'll say?" Suddenly he leaps over the table, grabs my elbows and runs me back into the wall. He presses against me, breathes in my ear. "I could kill you now."

"No. The cops. They'd find DNA!"

"There'll only be blood if you're cut." He licks my neck. "But I can strangle you with your panties. As for hairs, they'd be expected; everyone knows you've been here lots. The trunk of Mom's car could be a problem. But I'll shave your corpse and wrap it in a plastic sheet before I toss it in, dump it in a country ditch."

"Is that what you did to the other girls?"

"No. You're my first. Lucky you, eh?" He nuzzles my ear. "God, you're sweet."

I want to knee him, bite his cheek, but then he'd kill me for sure, so instead I yell.

"Shut up!" He punches the side of my head. "No one can hear you down here, so Just ... Shut ... Up!" His voice is worse than fists. I crumple to the floor, sobbing.

"Yeah. Cry for me, baby."

"You're sick!"

His mouth twists. "You have no idea." And now he backs away, breathing heavy, leans against the pool table. "Wake up, Leslie. You skip school, do drugs, act like a total ho. You're a bottom-feeder. Nobody cares what happens to you. So here's the story about tonight. You knew my family and I were away. You broke in. Stole money, jewelry, and hit the streets. Disappeared. A teen runaway. Happens every day."

I'm hyperventilating. "I left Mom a note. You'll get blamed if anything happens."

"Oh?" He grins. "You wrote her a lie to get me in trouble?"

"She'll call the cops. They'll come."

"We'll be long gone." He picks up a pool cue.

"They'll know it was you."

"They can know what they like. They'll never prove it." He strokes the pool cue. "Now on your feet. It's time for your lesson."

I get up, blubbering. Stand there while he looks me over.

"Okay, bitch," he says. "Strip."

I fumble my hands to the top button of my jeans. As soon as I take off my clothes, he'll kill me. I gotta do something, but what? I turn away, hunch over, pretend to unbutton. Dear God, let me live and I promise to be perfect from now on.

"Face me," he says.

My right hand slips into my pocket.

"I said turn around!" he barks. "Gimme a show!" He jabs me in the back with the end of the cue.

I start moving my shoulders up and down, like a stripper doing an act. Up and down, I wiggle towards him, up and down, still faced away.

"Yeah! Toss in some ass!"

Up and down, hand deep in my pocket. Up and down, hand searching. Up and down. I've found what I need.

"Face me, bitch!"

And I do. Fast. Hand out of my pocket. House keys clenched between my knuckles. I slash across his face full force. I rip an eyelid.

"Aaa!!!" He staggers back. "You'll pay for that!"

The tip of the pool cue whizzes by my ear. It slices the air again and again as he swings, blood in his eyes. "You're dead!"

I duck under the pool table as the cue smacks down. It cracks across the side pocket, snaps. I do a side-roll under the table, hop to my feet, run to the door and throw it open.

But he's behind me. Grabs my hair. Yanks me back. I'm on the table.

"You wanna play games?" He raises the broken end of the cue.

My hand's on a billiard ball. I pitch wild. It cracks

him in the mouth. Stunned, he falls back, howls. Charges again. Stabs the jagged cue end to the table.

"Die, bitch!"

But I've squirmed away. I'm up the stairs. I'm out the front door. I'm screaming all the way down the street.

Thirty-Four

Does anyone hear me?

If they do, I doubt they'll check. This is a nice, quiet neighborhood, where everyone minds their own business. That is, until the cops and ambulances show up, along with the TV cameras, and bodies get hauled off to the morgue. Then everyone acts all surprised. "Well, we heard something, but we thought it was kids horsing around." Or a cat. Or a car backfiring. Anything except somebody getting raped or beaten to death. Cuz that only happens other places. Not here.

I see myself on a porch, banging away, him coming, and the people inside bolting the door. "We don't want any trouble. Go away!" Is that what they'd really do? I don't know. But I can't afford to find out. I've got to get away from here now.

I glance over my shoulder, but Jason hasn't followed. Instead, he's closed his front door and turned off the lights, except for the fancy lantern by the steps. His house looks like every other house on the street. Even if people around here came to the window, what would they see? Some crazy girl screaming.

A bus pulls up as I hit the shelter. I flash my transit pass, head to the back and slouch down, so if Jason drives by I'll be hidden.

My mind races. How bad is his cut? Will it need stitches? Can he charge me with assault? Wouldn't that be a joke. But typical. So far, I don't even have a bruise. I wish I did. If I looked beat up, maybe somebody'd believe me. Or maybe not. Beachball'd say I did it to myself. She wouldn't be the only one. Practically the whole world would side with him. After all, the McCreadys are Somebodies. If it's my word against theirs, guess who wins?

I get to the subway. When I ran from Jason's house with the memory card, I felt safe underground. Not now. I picture him racing down to the platform, pushing me onto the rails. They'd call it an accident. I imagine the crowd watching as I'm hosed off the tracks, pissed I've delayed their ride.

Now things happen like in a dream. I know where I am and I know what I'm doing, but it's as if I'm somebody else, separate from my body, watching myself do things: getting on the train, going past my stop, transferring to the line that takes me to the commuter station downtown.

Who can I trust? Mom. Katie. Maybe Ms. James. Can they protect me? Don't make me laugh. He wants me dead. He knows where I live. He'll get what he wants.

Unless I go someplace he won't think about. Dad's.

I get off at the commuter station. The first thing I have to do is call home. Mom will be going wild.

I drop my last change into the pay phone. She picks up on the first ring. "Leslie?"

"Yeah."

"Where are you? What's happened?"

"Nothing," I say. "Everything's fine."

"*Fine?* You leave for the store—"

"Don't yell at me."

"Leslie, I want you back here this instant!"

"I can't. Something's come up."

"Leslie, now!"

"I said no. I'm not coming back! Not ever! Know why? Because you always yell at me!" I hang up and walk in circles, slapping my legs. Why is she like this? Then I'm ashamed. I've crapped up her life so bad. It'll be better for her with me gone. She'll see that once she's had time to cool down. It's sort of a silver lining.

I head outside to bum the money to get to Oakville.

These days, there's so much competition in the pan-handling department, it's hard to make a buck. An old guy, maybe forty, offers to help me out, wink, wink, but I shout in his face, "Does your wife know you're out screwing kids?" He takes off fast as the space shuttle.

I decide I need a sob story. "I'm a runaway. Please help me go home," I cry to anyone who'll listen. The first part is true, and the second part is sort of true, considering that "home" is what Dad and Brenda call Oakville. It goes to show that people can tell the truth and still be liars. Truth is complicated.

At last I meet this middle-aged woman. She's going a couple of cities farther, but says she'll buy me a ticket if I'll sit with her on the train. I figure this condition is to make sure I'm not lying about wanting the money for a ticket.

Well, that's only half of it. Turns out she's a Jehovah's Witness, so all the way to Oakville I'm listening to her talk about being saved. I want to tell her to take a hike. But me listening is making her day, so I just sit tight and chalk it up as a good deed.

As we pull into Oakville she gives me money for a cab to Dad's and a copy of the *Watchtower*, which she pulls from a small pile in her bag. I say thanks, and how someday I'll drop by the Kingdom Hall and get more information. Then I run.

Thirty-Five

I don't know what I expect from Dad. After the Brenda blowout, I told him that since he didn't have time for me Saturdays, I didn't have time for him Sundays. I only planned to make that punishment last a few weeks, but by then I was up to my ears in Jason.

Dad took me to lunch a couple of times. I ate fast, then said I had to go get ready for a date. He acted all smarmy, said he was happy I had a boyfriend and he'd leave it to me to let him know when I had time for a visit. By the time Jason and I broke up, I wasn't seeing him much.

I've called, but it's usually Brenda who's answered. Lately, Dad hasn't been home. "He's working late."

Like when he was working late with you? I want to laugh. Well, boo hoo. What you did to Mom, someone's doing to you. But that's not what I say. Instead, I go super sympathetic. "Gee, Brenda, I'm verrry, verrry sorry. You must be devastated." (That's way better—mean but polite, and points for vocab.) Then I hang up and picture her crying, all alone in what should have been Mom's and my apartment.

But this is the problem of doing-unto-others—drop a turd on somebody's plate and tomorrow you'll be eating their leftovers. That's what I'm thinking as I buzz Dad's apartment. Because now I'm the one with the problem and she's the one who gets to turn the screws.

"Who is it?" She's even Cute and Perky over the intercom.

"It's me. Is Dad there?"

"Dave, it's Leslie." Good, he's home for once. Bzzz.

I open the door and go to the elevator. The lobby doesn't smell so new anymore. But unlike at our place, the carpets aren't crusty, the windows are clean and there are real plants, not just green plastic dust magnets.

Dad and Brenda are waiting by the elevator door when it opens. He scoops me out and hugs me. "Leslie. Your mother called. You had us worried sick." He's so embarrassing when he tries to act like a father. I want to say, "Chill out." Instead, I hold on and cry. I don't care who sees.

We go to their apartment. Dad gets me settled in the kitchen and asks Brenda to make some hot chocolate while he phones Mom to say I've been found.

"I wasn't lost. And don't call Mom."

He kneels in front of my chair and holds my hands. "Leslie, we have to."

"Why can't I just stay here and nobody know?"

Dad looks at Brenda to see what to say, but for once she's smart and keeps her mouth shut. For once he's smart too. Instead of talking, he asks a question. "Leslie ... What's going on?"

The air chokes up my nose. "Nothing." An awful silence. He watches me sniffle. "It's just ... we always fight. She always yells. I don't want to be there. I want to be here with you."

Another awful silence.

"Leslie ... What's really going on?"

"Why? Don't you want me?"

"Of course we do. But right now, we need you to tell us the truth."

"You won't believe me."

"Trust us."

I gulp and give Brenda a look. She gets the message and leaves, giving Dad's shoulder a little rub as she passes. I look into his eyes. My lip trembles. I hear myself say, "A guy wants to kill me."

"What guy?"

In the background, I hear Brenda calling Mom. I don't care anymore.

"The guy I was going out with. Jason McCready. He knows where I live."

Dad takes this in. "Leslie," he says carefully, "sometimes people say things they don't mean."

"He's tried!"

"Leslie?" He gives me a questioning look.

"I knew you wouldn't believe me."

"I do." He doesn't. "Why don't we call his parents? Get to the bottom of this."

What a dork. I pull my hands away, cross my arms and start to rock.

"We can call the police, too," he adds fast. "Would that make you feel better? Maybe they can drop by, talk to him, straighten this out."

"No! Talking won't help."

Dad closes his eyes for a second, like I'm being difficult. Then he says, all gentle and earnest, "Leslie, what else can we do?"

"Nothing!" I look right at him. "Nothing! That's

what I've been trying to tell you! It's why I'm here! It's why you have to protect me!"

"Of course I'll protect you."

"You won't. You'll send me back to Mom!"

"Okay, okay." He clicks his tongue. "For tonight, how 'bout you sleep here in your room?" My room—that's what he calls the spare room when I'm around. "You get a good night's sleep and tomorrow we'll see what we can do."

Brenda shows up in the doorway. "I talked to Linda. She'll be here in half an hour," she says to Dad in this stage whisper, like maybe I'm deaf or something.

My eyes go wide.

"I'll call her right back," Dad reassures me, squeezing my hand. "Don't you worry. You're staying here."

"Dave?"

He shoots Brenda a glance. "Just deal with the hot chocolate, will you?" He picks up the phone on the wall by the fridge and punches in the number. "Linda, it's Dave." He must have got her just before she left.

Listening to one side of their conversation is hard. I keep wanting to add things, important things, but he keeps waving me down like he can handle it. Which he can't.

"Apparently, there's this young man ... Jason, right ... He's made a threat. She's scared sick ... I told her that ... Yes, I told her that ... Yes, I told her that too ... All right then. We'll see you in half an hour." He hangs up.

"You said I could stay here."

"You can. Your mother's just coming out. We all need to talk."

"She'll make me go back. She will. You'll let her."

"I won't."

"You will! And he'll kill me!"

"Leslie—"

"You liar! Coward!" And I bolt from the room and out the door.

Dad chases me down the hall. "Come back!"

Forget the elevator, stairs are faster. I fly like a bat out of hell. I hit the lobby and I'm gone.

Thirty-Six

It's cold this time of year, and I don't know where to go. I think of a bus shelter, to get out of the wind, but that's too obvious. Mom and Dad'll be driving around looking for me, with Brenda stuck "holding the fort." They'll have cops after me, too. In the city, big deal. There's lots of street kids, and hostels where I could give a fake name. But in places like this, the nomads stand out.

I end up hiding behind these evergreen bushes along the side of a school a couple of blocks away. They won't think to look for me here—it's too close. As a bonus, there's some heat coming from the building, and I can see the lights up in Dad's apartment.

I don't really sleep. My ears are so cold I think they're going to fall off, but when I pull my jacket up over my head my bum freezes. Around two in the morning, I think I see Mom's car drive by. Then around four I see the lights in Dad's apartment go out. I wonder if she's in the spare room.

By seven, it's getting light. I could hang around here and pretend to be a student, but not even browners get to school this early. If I don't head out soon I'll be spotted by a janitor come to turn on the boiler.

I crawl out from under the bushes. I'm stiff, I'm hungry, and my nose is running. I try hopping up and down to warm up. Some people think kids run away because it's cool, like we're all monkey-see-monkey-do. Right, we really want to get sick and dirty and starve to death because we saw somebody do it on TV.

A car pulls into the parking lot. A janitor. I take off.

I walk around for maybe an hour. Traffic starts up, people driving to work in the city. I wonder what Jason's doing, if he's back home waiting outside my apartment. And then I see this donut shop.

I go inside. At first I'm self-conscious, what with all the suits there to pick up a coffee and muffin. But soon I relax, on account of the grungies. There's this table of guys with hat hair who look like they're sobering up from an all-nighter. And a woman with so much makeup she's either a hooker or a beautician. And next to the door, this guy with shakes and tattoos who's tapping his feet like he's waiting for his dealer—and his dealer's really really late. Around these guys, I don't smell at all.

I take a seat, rub my hands together and think. What do I do for food? For money? Last night at the train station was a wakeup. Whenever I begged before, it was for fun, to see if I could do it, and I had way better luck. Usually enough for a movie within half an hour. It's weird, but wanting something so bad it hurts makes it harder to get.

Right now I need to eat. As soon as I'm warm I'll set up shop outside the front door and guilt the suits leaving for work. Then, in the afternoon, I can find a strip mall, beg outside an electronics store. That way I can watch the TVs through the window if I'm bored.

Someone's staring at me.

I look up in panic and see what passes for the manager—this twenty-something guy in a red-and-white striped shirt and a clip-on bow tie. His hair's all slicked back and he has a big Adam's apple. He points to a sign with block letters and announces in this official voice, "Tables for customers only."

"Thanks a lot," I go, all sarcastic, "but I can read, Dale."

He looks surprised, like he's thinking, How does she know my name?

I point at his name tag: "Hi, My Name Is Dale."

"I'm going to have to ask you to leave."

I pull out my wallet. "As a matter of fact, I'm here to order two dozen donuts for my dad. So you better apologize or he'll drop by later and talk to your boss."

Dale's face goes blotchy. "Sorry."

I give him a smirk and join the lineup. I'm glad it's long. I don't have any money and this way I have a while longer to warm up. Also to breathe in the cigarettes. There's so much smoke in here it's like puffing a pack.

"How may I help you?" I look up. It's "Hi, My Name Is Shirley."

I'm at the front of the line. How did that happen? I hear myself say, "I'll have six honey glazed, six walnut crullers, six chocolate glazed and six blueberry jelly, please."

All of a sudden, there's a box with two dozen donuts in front of me. I think about saying, These donuts are stale! and taking off. But they look so good and I'm so hungry I just grab the box and run.

Next thing I know, Shirley's yelling, suits are blocking the door, I'm being held by drunks and Dale's on the phone to the cops.

Thirty-Seven

Officer Maloney is fat with a notepad. He looks like the kind of guy who gets drunk and makes toasts at dinner parties. Officer Brant is his partner. She'd be okay if it weren't for the coffee breath. They're standing on either side of me out by the cruiser.

I'm too scared to look at their faces. Instead, I look at the windows of the donut shop. It seems we're quite the topic of conversation, everyone nodding at each other and pointing. As for Dale, he's strutting around like he'll be getting a medal from Crimestoppers or something.

Officer Brant does the talking. "Could you show us some ID?" She looks like a kickboxer.

"Don't have any." I shove my hands into my pockets and move from side to side. It's so cold.

"Do you have a name?"

"Uh, Melissa Johnson," I say.

"Well, 'Uh, Melissa Johnson,' could you give us your real name?" Officer Brant doesn't crack a smile, but I know she thinks she's funny. So does Officer Maloney.

"My name's Melissa Johnson," I repeat, more confident this time.

"Where do you live?"

"At 162 Cranberry Street."

"Never heard of it."

"Well, that's where I live." I feel the cold come up through my sneakers.

Officer Brant gets in my face. The reek of Maxwell House makes me gag. "It looks to me like you're underage."

"No way. I'm eighteen."

"When were you born?"

I get the year wrong. And I'm supposed to be good at math.

Now it's Officer Maloney's turn. "Look, 'Melissa,' either you tell us the truth or we arrest you for theft, vagrancy and interfering with a police investigation."

"Over two dozen donuts?"

Maloney flips his notepad shut and goes to the car radio. Officer Brant stands there, arms folded, and watches me cry.

"Please. They got them back. What more do you want? Just let me go."

Of course they don't. There's a Missing Persons bulletin matching my description. Talk about putting a move on. I heard somewhere cops normally wait a day after a person goes missing in case they're just sulking or something. It doesn't take much to figure Mom or Dad must have mentioned Jason and the death threat stuff.

They drive me to the station and put me in this room to wait for my parents. They also bring me some chicken noodle soup. It comes in a paper cup out of a machine, so it's pretty gross, but I don't care. Right now it tastes good.

Officers Maloney and Brant sit around and keep me company. Once they found out they'd got a missing person, they started acting different.

I guess that means I'm not going to jail. I don't feel like chatting, though. I just want to have my soup and be by myself. "You don't need to babysit me."

They don't take the hint. Instead, they make small talk. I guess they figure this is a chance to stay inside and get warm. I decide to tune out. I pretend I'm in physics. We wait forever for Mom and Dad, but when they walk in it feels like no time's passed at all.

I was afraid they'd be mad. But they aren't. They're serious. So serious nobody'd know they actually hate each other's guts.

Somebody else is with them. This woman in a navy dress suit. Maloney and Brant get up.

Mom doesn't wait for introductions. She comes over and hugs me. Then she and Dad shake hands with Maloney and Brant, and I get introduced to the new person, Detective Constable Sylvia Kissoon. She tells me to call her Sylvia. I don't really look at her, not to be rude or anything, but because I'm nervous.

"I'll take it from here," Sylvia says to Maloney and Brant. She asks my parents to wait while she talks to me privately in the room next door. I follow her over. We sit opposite each other with a table between us. Time goes so slow it's almost in reverse. Sylvia turns on a pocket recorder.

"Try to ignore this," she says.

Right. My palms are sweating. So are my feet. There's no air. I can't breathe. Sylvia catches my eye and holds it. She's smiling, friendly, but firm and controlled, like my old swimming instructor the first time I did the dog paddle across the pool.

Once I'm settled, she asks a few questions. Ordinary questions about how I am and can she get me anything, stuff like that, but I know where things are headed. I mean, she's not paid to be nice. This is to loosen me up so I'll let something slip.

I know all this, but even so, when the real questions come, I just answer. What's the point of hiding now? If she doesn't want to believe me, fine.

But it's not like she doesn't believe me. She keeps nodding, concentrating so hard it's like she's pulling the words out of me with her eyes.

I get scared. I say, "It's not like it's Mom's fault or anything. You're not going to give Dad custody or anything, are you?"

Sylvia shakes her head. "No, of course not." Then she smiles again and asks another question. I wonder if she's married. Or has kids. I wonder if she has problems with them, like Mom with me. And now I see she's staring at me waiting for an answer.

I talk and talk and talk. I talk about earlier, when me and Jason met and how the hitting started. And then she asks about Jason and sex.

I freeze. Sylvia keeps eye contact and waits.

"Look, if you really want to know, just read my journal."

"Your journal?"

Suddenly the world goes red alert.

Thirty-Eight

"Your journal will be evidence—key evidence—if Jason goes to trial," Sylvia says.

But the cops won't lay charges unless I cooperate. Court will be tough. Jason's lawyer will try to make me look like a liar. Even if Jason's found guilty, he won't get much time. He's barely eighteen, comes from a "good family" and hasn't been in trouble before. So for me to get dragged through crap seems pointless, especially when it could all be for nothing.

Sylvia and I talk about the other girls I saw on the porn files. She shows me photos of missing kids, but I don't recognize them. If only I hadn't destroyed the memory card!

"It wouldn't have changed much," Sylvia comforts. "The card isn't proof he took the shots. His lawyer could say he downloaded them when he was underage. What we need are the girls themselves. And the card wouldn't tell us who they are or how to find them."

Sylvia says I can wait to decide what to do. In the meantime, she hooks Mom and me up with Victim Services. We get deadbolts for our apartment, call display for the phone, plus I'm given a free cell to use if I'm alone and in trouble.

I also get to "see someone" who specializes in abuse. Her name is Dr. Seymour. She's written a book, which makes me think she must be smarter than the goof I went to for family counseling.

On the school front, Beachball is unsinkable. The cops ask her what she knew and when she knew it. Guess what? According to her, she had no idea there was a problem. Yes, she'd read my journal, and spoken to me immediately, but I told her it was make-believe. Cover your ass, Ms. Barker, it's big enough.

Beachball says that my missed exams won't count against me. My term work's good enough that I'll either scrape through or get failures bumped to a fifty. That hardly makes up for the fact that Jason gets to stay at the school; without charges there's no reason to expel him. Beachball says if I'd feel more comfortable somewhere else, she'll be happy to arrange a transfer. Nice. He tries to kill me, and I'm the one she wants to move.

Thirty-Nine

This morning Mom let me sleep in. Since I'm not back at school yet, I guess she figured there's no point torturing me. As usual, I stayed inside, deadbolt secured. I'm still too nervous to go out unless I'm with somebody. "Jason won't come after you while the heat's on," Katie says. Probably not, but crazier things have happened.

Anyway, I'm in front of the TV having breakfast—

a Coke and a slice of leftover pizza—when the phone rings.

It's Sylvia. "I've got something for you to look at. Do you have some free time?"

"Let me check my date book," I joke. Sylvia doesn't laugh. Twenty minutes later, she's at my kitchen table, pulling a surprise out of her briefcase.

At first I don't get it. Then it clicks. Sylvia may not have a sense of humor, but she sure is smart. I'm staring at a copy of last year's yearbook from Port Burdock Central High. Port Burdock—Jason's old stomping grounds. Jason was at the boys' academy, but there were girls at the town's public school.

I flip through the yearbook. Freeze. The girls' faces are magnets. Amber Bentham, 9C. Melanie Brady, 10B. They smile out at me from their class pictures, but their eyes have secrets. Strange. I thought I was done with crying.

I'm hyper all day till Katie runs over after class. We sit in the bathroom giving each other facials. Katie thought this'd be good for calming me down, seeing as it's a big sin to move your lips while the mask is drying.

I don't care. I talk like a bad ventriloquist. "I caaan't jussst sssit heeere waiiiting. I'vvve goooot tooo caaall theeem."

Katie shakes her head and writes on a piece of paper: "Let the police do it."

"Nooo waaay. I caaan't."

Katie writes: "Look in the mirror."

I do and burst out laughing. These aren't normal facials. They're Fun Facials, sleepover specials courtesy of Katie's mom. My face is this bright fluorescent orange; Katie looks like a cherry lollipop with hair.

"Yooour mooom isss meeentaaal!"

Katie giggles. Then she holds up her hand and shushes me while she stares at her watch for three minutes. Every time I go to say something, she kicks me.

"Oookaaay," she says at last. We wash our faces off, hers in the sink, mine in the bathtub. After we're done, we go back into the living room and I start up again.

"Leslie, get real," Katie says. "Calling those girls is the stupidest idea you've had in ages."

"Why? Don't you think they'd like to know they're not alone? I bet they don't even know about each other —and they're in the same school!"

"Leave it alone."

"And it'll all go away?"

"I didn't say that."

"Katie, please. I'll only do it if you say it's okay. Puh-leeaasse? For meeeee?? Puh-llleeeeeaaaaasssssse???"

Her eyes bug. "How does your mom put up with you?"

I grab her hand and yank her to the computer in the living room. We go online to the directory, my heart doing loop-de-loops. Luckily Port Burdock's not too big. There's just five Bradys and two Benthams.

I call the first Bentham and put on the speaker phone so Katie won't bug me about what's going on. A boy answers. There's the sound of a TV in the background. "Yeah?"

He sounds little, but just in case, I put on my polite voice. "Hello, this is Leslie Phillips. Could I please speak to Amber?"

The boy yells, "It's for you," and I hear this voice yell back, "I'll take it in my room." I've hit the jackpot, first try. The boy doesn't say anything else, but I can still hear the TV. Finally the other voice comes on the line.

"Hello?"

So this is Amber Bentham, the girl in 9C. She must be in grade ten now. My grade. To think I know her phone number, where she lives, goes to school—what she looks like naked—and she doesn't even know I exist.

"Hello," I reply. It's all I get out.

"You can hang up," Amber says into the phone to her brother. Pause. I can still hear the TV. "I said, you can hang up now, Jeffrey!" Click. "So, hi. Who is it?"

"Leslie Phillips. You don't know me, but I know you, sort of. At least, I know Jason McCready."

Her voice gets small. "Who did you say you were?"

"Leslie Phillips. I'm nobody. Just this girl. I went out with him."

I thought being humble, a kindred spirit or something, would make her friendly. Instead, she acts like me on a bad day. "Well, maybe you went out with him, but I didn't, and if you're the one who ratted my name to the cops, I don't know how you know who I am, but they were just here, and you got me in trouble with my parents, so thank you very much, and don't ever call me again." She hangs up.

"Katie," I say, "is it a sin to do something bad for a good cause?"

"I think so."

"Then say a prayer for me." I phone back. Amber answers. Before she can hang up again, I say, "Amber, I have the sex pix. If you don't talk to me I'm going to e-mail them to your dad and the town newspaper."

"Oh god."

She's so scared, I'm ashamed of myself. "What happened to you also happened to me," I say. "I want to charge him, but officially he's a first-time offender. If you charge him too, maybe we can put him away longer."

There's a pause. "Has anyone else seen the pictures?"

"No. They're on a memory card. Nowhere else."

"Thank you. Thank you." She's practically kissing my feet over the phone line. "Promise me you'll destroy the card."

"Not till you agree to help me."

"I can't!"

"Yes, you can," I say firmly.

"It's different for you." Her voice cracks. "He doesn't live here anymore. I'm finally getting some sleep."

"No, you're not. He's in your head. He keeps waking you up."

"How do you know?"

"I just do." I hear her sob. I wish I could hug her.

"When that detective showed up at the door, I didn't know what it was all about." She blows her nose. "She got me alone in the living room and asked me all these questions: if I knew Jason, if he'd hurt me, if he'd raped me. I felt like a criminal. She said if I ever remembered anything to give her a call. After, she told my folks I hadn't done anything wrong, but they acted like they didn't believe her. Mom kept saying, 'We've never had trouble with the police.'" Amber whispers: "Look, it was the end of last year. I remember him taking the photos, but not much else. I'd never had more than a glass of wine at Christmas dinner before that. I thought I was going to bleed to death. I tried to break up with him, but he wouldn't go away. Finally he went on a date with Jenny Maraida to make me jealous."

I get chills. "Who's Jenny Maraida?"

"You don't know? Her dad caught them drunk and naked in the family garage. He called the principal at the academy and Jason got booted out for what they called 'drunkenness and other grave misdemeanors.' If it was anybody but Dr. Maraida reporting him, nothing would have happened. I mean, the guys at the academy are rich kids in jackets and ties. They walk through town like they own the place."

"Back to Jason."

"No." Amber stops me cold. "I haven't seen him

since. I never want to again. There must be somebody else who can help you."

"There is," I sigh. "A girl from your school named Melanie Brady."

"Jason went out with Melanie?"

"Once, anyway. I'll try her instead."

A terrible pause. "You can't."

"Why not?"

"Melanie Brady is dead."

Forty

Melanie Brady committed suicide.

According to Amber, one morning before the bell, the halls at her school were alive with whispers. The kind that spread faster than flu. Apparently Melanie'd posted porn shots of herself on her Facebook page. She'd also Hotmailed the pix to her entire address book. Someone had taped up a printout in the guys' washroom, and a couple of her so-called friends were flashing copies hidden in their binders.

Melanie wasn't at school to defend herself. Kids were saying she should hide her face forever, she's such a slut. That talk stopped with the morning announcements. The principal said there'd been a tragedy: Melanie Brady was dead.

All morning, guidance counselors dealt with weeping

classmates who'd never had time for Melanie when she was alive. (As Amber tells me this, I have a flash of Ashley. If I died, she'd be first in line to get attention. No, I take it back. When a person's dead, lots changes, and the rest doesn't matter.)

By lunch, the word was out that Melanie'd swallowed sleeping pills and slit her wrists in the bathtub. Amber says everyone had questions: Was Melanie a secret druggie? Had she posted when she was high, then killed herself when she realized what she'd done? Kids who knew her said she was weird and impulsive. But this went too far to make sense even to them.

"Well, it makes sense to me," I say. "You too, right? We know Jason. I'll bet anything Melanie broke up with him. He had her password and went to an Internet café. He logged on to her Facebook page, wiped out her privacy settings and posted her file from his memory card. Then, in case the post got taken down, he sent the stuff through her e-mail account too. Sound about right?"

"So? We can't prove it." Amber chokes up. "You know, he threatened to do the same to me when I left him. I changed my password, but twice a week he'd call or text: 'Today's the day.' That's all he'd say, but I knew what he meant. The messages stopped when he moved away. But I'm still afraid. Please, please destroy my photos!"

I don't have the heart to blackmail her anymore. "They're history," I say. "I burned the memory card ages ago."

There's a shudder of relief. "Thank you." A deep breath. "Look, about the trial. I wish I could help, but I can't. My dad's real conservative. Mom too. I'm supposed to be perfect. They'd die."

"Right," I say.

"Forgive me?"

"I don't know." I hang up.

Katie gives me a back rub. We stare out the window. After a while, she gets bored and starts to paint my toenails. I stop her before she puts smiley faces on the big toes with Liquid Paper. She sighs and gets out her sparkle dust instead, like she's Tinkerbell on happy pills or something.

"Not now!" I say, and yank my foot away. Katie thinks I'm mad. But I'm not. I'm just very, very determined. "Katie," I say, "I'm having Jason charged."

"Are you serious? You'll be all by yourself."

"I don't care. I won't live in fear like Amber. I won't run away. Not ever again." I hold her hand. "Without the other girls coming forward, Jason won't get what he deserves. But, Katie, if I let him get away, the next time he does it, he'll still be Mister Perfect. At least if I say what he did out loud in court his name will be on the record. There'll be a trail. A history."

"What if he tries to get even?"

"He can come after me no matter what I do. But each time he's gotten away with things, he's gotten worse. This is my only way to fight back."

"What if the judge doesn't believe you?"

"That's the least of my worries." I laugh at the truth of it.

Katie gasps like I've lost my mind. "You're either the bravest or the stupidest person I know, maybe both," she says. "But I'm with you no matter what."

That night, Mom tells me the same thing, except she leaves out the "stupid" part.

Me, I'd leave out the "brave" part, too. It's like, after talking to Amber, I realize there's no choice. Not for me. Not for what I want to be, or what I want to see when I look in the mirror.

Forty-One

When I say I'll testify, the police lay charges against Jason for rape, stalking, creation of child porn, forcible confinement and uttering death threats. He gets bail, but there's a bunch of catches. He can't make contact or be anywhere near me. That means I don't have to change schools, *he* does. And when he isn't at school, he has to be at home. To make sure he obeys, his parents have to put up a huge security bond, and he has to wear an electronic ankle bracelet. Talk about the GPS chip being on the other foot, eh?

With Jason out of the picture, I go back to school. Instead of running to the bathroom to cry all the time, I feel like I'm ten feet tall—I can take on the world. Who'd ever have guessed that going to school would make me feel so good?

It's especially fun watching Beachball suck up to me. Every time she sees me, she acts concerned and asks if there's anything she can do to help. (Like, go flush herself down the toilet?) My teachers give me extra breaks too. Guidance has sent them a memo to take my "difficult situation" into consideration. Even Mr. Manley has laid off.

Ms. James is ecstatic. The first time she saw me in the hall, she tried to give me a high five. Please. I backed off, but left her a note in her staff mailbox saying thanks. The students are something else again. You'd think I was a celebrity. Girls who used to ignore me come up to say I'm amazing and should get an award or something. Right. They're basically looking for dirt. Meanwhile, guys make a point of steering clear, as if they think I'll charge them with harassment if they peek at my boobs.

Nicky Wicks was really funny. He came up all sweaty and smelly and said he was sorry he used to look up my skirt. "How interesting," I said, trying not to laugh. You should have seen him shake.

Forty-Two

After a preliminary hearing, Jason goes to trial. The prosecutor, Mr. Pérez, has lined up the psychiatrist I've been seeing, Dr. Seymour; she'll testify for us as an expert on child abuse. But Jason's lawyer has a psychiatrist too, who's apparently going to say I'm a chronic liar. Katie wanted to testify about my bruises, the photos Jason took of us in the park and seeing me burn the memory card. Unfortunately, Mr. Pérez told us, none of that's evidence, just hearsay: Katie didn't see me get hurt, those photos are innocent and she never saw what was on the card.

"The case is a toss-up," Mr. Pérez warns me. "The verdict will all depend on who the court believes: you or Jason."

"So I'm on trial too."

"In a way," he nods. "Good luck."

When the time comes, I take the stand and swear an oath to tell the truth. Mr. Pérez has me read aloud from my journal. It's embarrassing, but the pages keep me focused, so I don't have to look at Jason or his family.

That changes when Jason's lawyer, Mr. Addison, gets up to cross-examine me. Mr. Addison's an old guy with a silver mustache. He acts all folksy, but the whole time he's out to trip me up. I pretend he's Vice-principal Manley. People are a lot less scary when you're counting their nose hairs.

All the same, his questions are hard: "Do you agree you have quite an imagination, Leslie?" "How did you feel when Jason left you for Ashley?" "According to your own journal, you have a history of lying. Why should we believe you now?" "Again, according to your journal, you smoked a lot of marijuana. Why should we trust your memory?"

I try to concentrate, but I can't. I glance over at Jason. He smirks. Behind him, his parents burn holes through me with their eyes, like I'm a psycho liar out to ruin their family.

Against the McCreadys, I feel like trash. I'm about to lose control, then I look at my parents. Dad's supporting me in the back row with Brenda. But Mom's right at the front. She sits there, shoulders straight, chin up, so proud of me I can taste it. I won't let her down. I won't let myself down either.

I think of the girls on Jason's files—Melanie especially—and suddenly this power takes root inside me. It grows down to my toes and up to my brain, till every part of my body feels alive. I face Jason. I stare deep into his eyes. Now *he* looks away.

I turn back to Mr. Addison. I answer his questions in a clear, calm voice. I tell the truth. All of it.

Jason takes the stand right after me. He says he can't apologize for something he hasn't done, and he can't understand why I'm doing this; at the time, he thought I'd taken his breaking up with me pretty well. Mr. Pérez goes at him hard, but Jason holds his ground, all earnest and sincere. When he's finished, he slips me a wink.

But even Jason can't keep his cool when he gets the verdict: Guilty on all counts.

Forty-Three

If I was making a movie, I'd have Jason sentenced to the pen for years, screaming for mercy as he's hauled away to a prison crawling with rats. I'd put him in a cell with a maniac who tortures him day and night the way he tortured me and the others.

If I was a nicer person, I'd have him getting therapy and leaving prison a whole new guy, seeking forgiveness and never doing another awful thing in his life. To be super cheesy, I'd maybe have him devote the rest of his life to charity.

But this isn't a story. It's the truth. And the truth isn't like that.

Jason's father doesn't show up for the sentencing, but his mother's there, dressed in black and wearing shades. She's like a zombie. So is Jason. I'd imagined he'd at least be shaking, but he's so controlled it's frightening. When the judge asks if he has a statement to make, he says, "Only one thing, Your Honor. I'm innocent."

The judge adjusts his glasses, and rips into him for what he's done and his failure to apologize. "I hope you'll reflect on your actions while in jail, and learn to take responsibility for your life," he says.

Jason gets two years. Plus, since he's eighteen, his name goes on a sex offenders registry, and a sample of his DNA is put on file. Once released, he'll have to let police know where he's living. It'll be easier to catch and convict him if he ever does anything again.

I watch as he's hauled away.

Forty-Four

"**I**'m still not sure what controls events, destiny or choice. All I know is, ever since I stood up for myself, I've felt good."

I'm talking to Ms. Graham. We bumped into each other by accident in the frozen foods section at the supermarket. I was hoping to pass by unrecognized, but her cart got stuck in the middle of the aisle. Next thing I knew she was staring at me with this funny look. "Leslie Phillips," she exclaimed. "Three years ago. Middle row, fourth row back."

It's weird seeing her outside of school, like she actually has a life. We talk for I don't know how long. About her early retirement. About Jason's trial. My life since. And all the things I used to think about in her class.

I tell her how sorry I am for the way we misbehaved.

"Not you," Ms. Graham says. "You never dropped your books. I remember."

As she's about to leave for the canned goods, I hear myself say, "Ms. Graham, I owe you so much. Without you, I wouldn't have had a journal. That journal was the evidence that convicted him. I want you to know, you made a huge difference in my life."

For a second, it's like the sun comes out across her face. "Thank you," she beams. She tugs at the end of her sweater, grips her cart handle and disappears.

My journal.

I still write in it. Dr. Seymour says it's therapeutic. I've needed that help in the time since Jason's been out. They tell me he's gone west. Dr. Seymour says I've probably seen the last of him. I'll never know for sure, but the fact he's moved away is a good sign. With our history, the registry and his DNA, it'd be risky for him to come after me. In the end, Jason's the world's biggest coward. And he knows I fight back.

Still, I think of all the other girls out there with a Jason. Girls living in fear and shame. Every so often, I close my eyes and try to send them strength. Katie calls it praying. I call it mental telepathy. Either way, I figure it can't hurt.

"You were so crazy back then," Katie says, fiddling with her lip gloss. "I mean, really, you should write a book. Let other girls know they're not alone. You could do it easy. Just fix up what you wrote. Call it *Leslie's Journal* or something."

I smile. Who knows? Maybe I will.

Thanks

This revised edition of *Leslie's Journal* is a thorough update of the original, incorporating the latest technology and the theme of cyber bullying.

In reworking the novel, I am particularly indebted to Staff Inspector Elizabeth Byrnes, who heads the Toronto Police Service Sex Crimes Unit, and to her colleagues Detective Constables Janet Sullivan and Marco Ricciardi (child exploitation), Detective Constable Marilyn White (threat assessment) and Detective Staff Sergeant Gordon Whealy (behavioral assessment).

As a Luddite whose computer skills are essentially limited to word processing, I'm also grateful beyond measure for the vetting of techno wizards Stephen Dow, Shelley Johnston, Christine Baldacchino and Alexander Blake-Davies.

I'd also like to thank again those professionals who helped with the original: Dr. Harvey Armstrong of Parents for Youth, counselor Terry Graham, lawyer Christine Milne, Detective Inspector Tony Warr, Detective Constable Tracey Marshall, Detective John Relph and publisher Rick Wilks and editor Barbara Pulling from Annick Press.

Finally, my heartfelt appreciation to friends Victoria Stewart, Louise Baldacchino, Dean Cooke, Jon Pearce, Daniel Legault, Patricia Ocampo, and Dan, Betty and

Laura Milne; to former students Yvonne Czerny, Norah Love, Laura Nanni and Suzanne Smith; and to all the Leslies in the world, who humble me with their strength and courage.